THE SHOWDOWN

D1548782

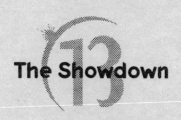

The Showdown

LEFT BEHIND
>THE KIDS<

Jerry B. Jenkins

Tim LaHaye

WITH CHRIS FABRY

TYNDALE HOUSE PUBLISHERS, INC.
WHEATON, ILLINOIS

Visit Tyndale's exciting Web site at www.tyndale.com

Discover the latest Left Behind news at www.leftbehind.com

Published in association with the literary agency of Alive Communications, Inc., 7680 Goddard Street, Suite 200, Colorado Springs, CO 80920.

Edited by Curtis H. C. Lundgren

ISBN 0-8423-4294-X

Printed in the United States of America

08 07 06 05 04 03 02 01
10   9   8   7   6   5   4   3   2

To Colin Andrew

TABLE OF CONTENTS

What's Gone On Before

JUDD Thompson Jr. and the other kids in the Young Tribulation Force are having the adventure of a lifetime. The vanishing of their families has left them alone. Now a global earthquake has scattered them.

After narrowly surviving a crash and a flood, Judd helps an injured biker and begins his long trip home. He decides to jump a motorcycle over a swollen river, but an aftershock plunges the cycle into the water and leaves Judd hanging on the edge of a bridge.

Vicki Byrne watches her principal, Mrs. Jenness, die before her eyes. When Vicki finally makes it home, she can't find Ryan Daley.

Lionel Washington is nearly killed by a collapsing building at a Global Community compound. A head injury wipes out his memory. Now he's in the hands of the GC and ready to serve Nicolae Carpathia.

Ryan is rescued, but an emergency shelter

nurse gives him bad news. Clinging to life, Ryan desperately tries to get a message to his friends.

In the aftermath of the great earthquake, the kids struggle to find each other and keep fighting the enemies of God.

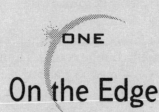

ONE

On the Edge

JUDD clung to a steel railing as the motorcycle disappeared into the river. He tried to climb the side but knocked more concrete from the edge. If Judd didn't hang on, it meant certain death. He cried for help.

The shaking stopped. Then came a splattering in the woods. *Tick, tick, tick.* He wondered if this was another judgment of God. Then something hit his head. Raindrops, slowly, then pouring.

Judd slipped and nearly let go. The rain beat fiercely. A steel support lay between him and the river. He didn't want to hit that on the way down.

His strength was giving out.

Judd tried once more and found something firm with his feet. He was almost to safety when the slab gave way and tumbled into the water. He fell back, his hands barely grasping the railing. Judd closed his eyes and gritted his teeth, but he couldn't hold on.

As he let go, someone grabbed his arm.

The room felt ice-cold. Everywhere Vicki saw sheet-draped bodies on tables. A hand stuck out from the body in front of her. She willed herself to pull the sheet back. The face was chalky white.

Ryan.

Dead.

Vicki screamed as she awoke. Darrion and Vicki sat up in the small tent.

"What's wrong?" Darrion said.

Through the flap Vicki watched men carrying bodies. The earthquake was over. Fires dotted the campsite, casting an eerie glow.

"Nightmare," Vicki said. "Where's Shelly?"

"Somebody came and asked for volunteers," Darrion said. "Shelly said to let you sleep."

Vicki scurried out of the tent, still wearing the same tattered clothes from the morning.

"Where are you going?"

"I have to find Ryan."

Shelly raced toward them. "Good news," she said. "A lady says they've opened a shelter a few blocks from here. It's the closest one to your house, so Ryan might be there."

"Let's go," Vicki said.

"We have to wait till dawn," Shelly said. "They're shooting looters."

"I don't care," Vicki said. "I have to find him."

"We don't need another death," Shelly said. "Get some sleep and we'll find him in the morning."

Vicki dragged herself back to the tent and tried to sleep, but she kept seeing the white, chalky face in her dream.

Lionel turned the gun over beside him on the bed. The GC insignia was engraved on the barrel of the pistol. He had signed papers that made him a Global Community Morale Monitor. He felt proud, but at the same time, things didn't seem right.

"I thought you'd be asleep by now," Conrad said, sitting next to Lionel's bed.

"Looks like you're going to be my partner," Lionel said.

"Guess so."

"You don't seem too excited," Lionel said.

"I don't know what I'm supposed to feel," Conrad said. "Everything's changing so fast. And that stuff in your luggage has me spooked."

"What stuff?" Lionel said.

"The Bible and your journal," Conrad said. "I can't wait to get on the Internet and see if this rabbi guy will answer me."

"Maybe when we get to Chicago, we'll figure it out," Lionel said.

The man Judd had talked with on the mountain pulled him to safety. His forearm was huge, and he easily lifted Judd over the side.

"Let's get out of here before another aftershock," he yelled over the rain.

Back in the cave the man handed Judd a blanket and sat him near a fire. "We watched you from up here. You almost made it over."

"I should have waited," Judd said.

Judd was exhausted. The frightened-looking people in the cave were lucky the rocks hadn't fallen on them.

The man introduced himself as Tim Vetter. His wife was a small woman named Marlene. Tim introduced Judd then asked, "Why were you out here? Trying to get to Chicago?"

Judd wasn't sure what he should tell them. If they were somehow linked with the Global Community, he should keep quiet.

"I was traveling with a friend," Judd stammered. "He didn't make it."

"That wasn't your bike, was it?" Tim said.

"I borrowed it," Judd said.

The other men laughed. "There's not much difference between stealing and borrowing during an earthquake," one man said.

"Tell the truth," Tim said.

"I helped a guy out, and he told me to take it," Judd said.

Was God preparing Vicki to face the death of one of the Young Trib Force? She tried to shake the idea but couldn't.

The birds were out again the next morning, singing in the few trees left standing. It seemed strange that all the sounds were perfect when the sights were so awful. She and her friends passed smoldering craters and collapsed buildings. Car taillights stuck out of the ground. Moaning and crying still came from the rubble.

The shelter was an apartment complex where workers had cleared plants and furniture from the atrium. Vicki told a guard holding a clipboard that she was looking for her brother. The guard showed them a list of names. On another sheet was a list of numbers for those who had not yet been identified. Some numbers were crossed out and had the word "deceased" written beside them.

Shelly pointed to a description. "This could be him."

A nurse led them to a storage room filled with beds. In the corner lay someone staring at the wall, a white bandage covering his head.

Vicki looked at Darrion and Shelly.

"You can do it, Vick," Shelly said.

"He can't talk," the nurse said.

Vicki approached warily. The face was covered except for holes for his eyes, nose, and mouth. His left arm was bandaged as well, and Vicki realized he had been badly burned.

"Ryan?" Vicki said.

The kid stared at the wall.

Vicki knelt beside him. "Ryan, it's Vicki," she said.

The boy shook his head. He motioned for pen and paper. "Not Ryan," he wrote.

Vicki sat staring at him.

"Go away," the boy wrote.

Vicki wiped away a tear. "I'm sorry you were hurt," she said.

Vicki asked the nurse if there was anywhere else Ryan could have been taken.

"A furniture store somehow made it through," the woman said. "A couple hundred survivors are there. More than we can handle."

People stirred in the cave as Judd awoke. The men huddled around the fire. Tim motioned for Judd to come and eat.

Judd was sore and had scratches from skidding on the bridge. He ate hungrily.

"Some of us are going back to look for food," Tim said. "There might be a relief site set up by the Global Community."

Judd flinched. "I wouldn't be surprised."

"Will you come with us?" Tim said.

"Think I'll try to keep going," Judd said.

Tim scratched at the embers with a stick. "There's something you're not telling us," he said. "It may be none of our business. But when you share our food and shelter, I think we deserve to know what's up."

"You've been very kind," Judd said. "I owe you my life."

Judd wondered if this was why he hadn't been able to complete the jump. Maybe God wanted him to tell his story, despite the risk.

"My name is Judd Thompson," he began.

Lionel took tests and signed more papers in the morning. Though the earthquake had knocked out communication and travel, the Global Community rolled on. A GC doctor declared Lionel fit and ready to continue his classes. Conrad stopped by as the doctor left.

"I don't understand," he said. "Thousands are dead or dying, but the GC has everything set up and ready to go. It's like they expected this."

"That's not possible," Lionel said.

"What if it is? Maybe they were waiting for some kind of disaster to put their next plan in motion. That would explain why they're so hot to get us out of here and on the job."

Conrad showed Lionel his gun, standard issue for Morale Monitors. "Why do they trust kids our age with guns?"

"Maybe when they see how you shoot this afternoon at the range, they won't," Lionel said, smiling.

The girls wound through neighborhoods, taking shortcuts through what had been backyards. They climbed over huge mounds of dirt and rocks, then went around craters. Smoke from the still-burning meteors made them choke.

The furniture store was on the way to the

Edens Expressway, a few minutes' drive away. But with downed utility poles, flattened buildings, pavement that had disappeared, and the girls on foot, it took much longer.

Shelly pointed to a neon sign on the ground. "My mom and I used to eat at that place," she said.

Vicki knew the furniture store. She had been there with her family. The sales staff had eyed them suspiciously, as if they knew she lived in a trailer and had neither the money nor the room for the bedroom set she wanted.

Only the roof of the building was visible. The rest had been swallowed whole. Rescue crews filed in and out, but there was no hurry. Everyone taken from the building was in a body bag.

"This could be a wild-goose chase," Shelly said. "What if he's not there?"

"We're gonna find him and take him home with us," Vicki said.

"How?" Shelly said. "What if he can't walk? We gonna carry him?"

"I'll find a way," Vicki said.

The furniture store was still standing, but there were no roads around it. Emergency vehicles pulled as close to the front as they could, then unloaded more injured.

"Most look pretty healthy," Vicki said. "Maybe Ryan's not that bad."

"We've got another problem," Darrion said.

Vicki gasped when she saw Global Community guards at the entrance. Only the injured and those with clearance cards were getting through.

The girls split up, then met again a few minutes later.

"The back is guarded too," Shelly said.

"The side doors are locked," Darrion said. "There's a lot of smashed windows, but they're too high to crawl through."

"We'll have to get in another way," Vicki said, smearing mud on her forehead. She tore off a piece of her shirt.

"What are you doing?" Shelly said.

Vicki lay on the ground. "Carry me," she said. "And I expect some tears from you two!"

Shelly smiled. She grabbed Vicki's arms, and Darrion took her legs.

Vicki moaned. Shelly and Darrion began crying as they neared the store.

A Global Community guard stopped them at the entrance. "You can't bring her here."

"You have to help," Shelly said. "We have to get her to a doctor."

Darrion kept her back to the guard so he

wouldn't recognize her. Shelly wept bitterly. "Please help us," she cried.

"All right," the guard said. "Put her down."

Vicki rolled her eyes and winked at them.

TWO

Finding Ryan

Vicki closed her eyes when the men carried her inside. She wailed when they sat her in a line of injured people. A Global Community staff worker took information. When she turned her back, Vicki quickly slipped out of line and down the hall. She ran up a flight of stairs.

What had been a showroom now held cots. People were sleeping, some badly wounded.

Vicki didn't want to risk talking with anyone, so she stayed out of the way. The doctors and nurses were so busy, no one seemed to notice her.

She looked at faces, read names on charts, and darted into a bathroom when a GC guard passed.

A woman in one of the stalls was crying. Vicki found a clipboard on a sink. At the top of the chart were numbers. Under "T-1" she spotted "Ryan Daley."

What's T-1?

The woman came out of the stall. Vicki washed her face, then quickly walked out.

As she hurried down a narrow corridor, she heard someone behind her, then felt a hand just above her elbow.

"You are under arrest."

Judd watched the group as he told his story. They didn't react strongly but seemed interested in what he thought of the disappearances. He told them what had happened to his family, about meeting Bruce Barnes, and about watching the videotape the former pastor had made.

"Before, I thought church was a stuffy place that didn't want you to have fun. They told you everything you weren't supposed to do. Now I see it as a place of life. God wanted me to know him. If anyone wants what I found, I can help you."

Tim looked at the other men and nodded. "We know what we have to do," he said.

The men dragged Judd to a corner of the cave. He struggled but couldn't overcome them. They tied his hands behind him.

"We were warned about people like you,"

one man said. "People like you are against Nicolae Carpathia. You're against the Enigma Babylon Faith."

"I didn't say anything about Carpathia," Judd said.

"You didn't have to," the man said.

Judd shook his head. His gut reaction about the people had been right.

"We're taking you back to town," Tim said. "We'll turn you over to the GC."

"For telling you about God?" Judd said.

"You must be running from something," Tim said, "or you wouldn't have taken such a chance. If you're innocent, the GC will let you go."

The group walked Judd down the hillside with his hands tied. He would soon be back in the hands of the enemy of his soul.

The men left Judd near the Enigma Babylon church building under the watch of Tim's wife, Marlene.

"We'll be back with food and water and the GC," Tim said.

A chill ran down Vicki's spine and she turned, thinking she would see a Global Community guard. But a wild-eyed young man with stringy hair, eyes darting, said,

"Scared you, didn't I? You thought I was the police. Not supposed to be in here, are you?"

Vicki took a breath. "Do you always ask that many questions?"

The young man smiled, still looking away.

"What's your name?" Vicki said.

"Charlie, Charles, Chuck, Charlie." He spoke quickly, and his body seemed out of control.

"You scared me, all right," Vicki said. "You like scaring people?"

Charlie giggled. His teeth were crooked and discolored. "I like when they jump. I used to make my sister jump. Real high. She don't jump no more. Big shake got her."

"The earthquake?" Vicki said.

"Yeah, yeah," Charlie said. "Earthshake. Lotsa things got broken at our house. Big crash. Boom!"

Charlie screamed and laughed, and Vicki jumped.

"Be quiet," Vicki said.

Charlie put a finger to his lips. "Shh. Quiet."

"Are you a patient here?" Vicki said.

"No, my sister worked here. They had big TVs downstairs. Used to let me watch them. All busted now. Want to see 'em?"

Vicki shook her head. "I'm looking for a friend who might be here."

"Friend. I had a friend. His mom said I was strange, and he couldn't come over anymore."

"I'll be your friend," Vicki said. "I just need your help."

"I can help," Charlie said. "I can lift and carry stuff and hold doors open and SCARE PEOPLE!"

"Stop screaming," Vicki said. "There are sick people in here. Now I'm trying to find room T-1, or something like that."

Charlie squinted and squeezed his chin. "Is a *T* the letter that looks like a snake?"

"That's an *S*," Vicki said. She drew a *T* in the dust on a window.

"I know what a *T* looks like," Charlie giggled. "Come on."

He hopped along, taking big leaps with his right leg and dragging his left behind him. When Vicki finally caught him, he was out of breath and excited.

"Right here," Charlie said.

The sign above the door said Trauma 1.

Charlie opened the door slowly. "There's really sick people here. Better not be too loud."

Bright children's furniture lined the wall. Vicki passed cribs and strollers.

"Stay close," Vicki said.

Judd sat in the rubble of the Enigma Babylon church, now both hands and feet tied. He could tell the church had once been beautiful, but its stained glass windows lay in pieces. After all his work to escape, Judd was almost back in the hands of the Global Community. He had hoped the GC would find the van destroyed and assume he was dead.

Marlene Vetter paced, looking at Judd, then glancing away.

Judd rubbed his ankles together, trying to loosen the rope. The rope around his wrists was already loosening.

"How long have you lived here?" Judd said.

The woman looked like she had a secret. "I'm not supposed to talk to you."

"Why?" Judd said. "I'm dangerous?"

"What you say is dangerous," Marlene said. "Look where it got you."

"The things I say are true. I don't care where it gets me."

The more Judd talked, the more Marlene looked away. That gave Judd a chance to work free of the ropes. Finally Marlene said, "You really believe all those things?"

Judd spoke carefully. "The vanishings, the earthquake, the meteors, all that was predicted in the Bible."

Marlene shook her head. "I'm talking about God forgiving you without you doing anything but admitting what you did. I always thought if your good outweighed your bad that God, whoever he was, would eventually accept you."

"Is that what Enigma Babylon teaches?" Judd said.

Marlene sat and pulled her knees to her chest. "They say God is within us. We don't need to be 'saved' from anything but our own low self-esteem."

"What do you think?" Judd said. "Does that make sense?"

"I'm not sure anymore."

Judd kept working at the ropes.

Someone yelled for Charlie.

"Oh," he said, "I'll stay with you."

"No," Vicki said. "Go so they don't suspect anything. Promise you won't tell them about me."

"I promise," he said, scampering off giggling.

Vicki strained to see the patients in the darkened room. Several had died, and sheets covered them.

Vicki heard the familiar beeps of monitors

scattered throughout the room. Finally, toward the end of one row, she saw Ryan. She rushed to him and ran a hand through his hair. It was caked with mud. His eyes were closed, and a bruise showed on his forehead.

Vicki's tears fell on Ryan's face. She hugged him, but he felt cold. She stepped back in horror. Vicki felt for a pulse.

Someone took Vicki by the shoulder. "What are you doing in here?" a woman said.

Marlene looked at Judd. "I've tried to believe like I should, but it doesn't work."

"You want me to go through it again?" Judd said.

Marlene nodded.

Judd explained that even though people are sinners, Jesus had died for them. "The only way to God is through Jesus, not through doing good things or believing in yourself. He created us. Sin separates us from God. To become his child, we have to be adopted into his family."

"But only if you're perfect?"

"I'm not perfect by a long shot," Judd said. "Ask my friends. But when God forgives you, Jesus lives in you. God doesn't see me and my faults. He sees Jesus."

"So I don't have to do anything?"

"You accept what God gives," Judd said.

Marlene stared off and shook her head. "Tim would kill me if he knew I talked to you."

Judd finally freed his hands from the rope.

"What you say sounds good," Marlene said, "but I don't know if I can trust you."

"Trust me," Judd said, showing her his hands. "I could free my legs and be out of here in seconds."

"Why don't you?"

"God's working on you," Judd said. "I can't leave you now."

Judd heard footsteps and hid his hands behind his back.

Vicki jumped back, turning to face the woman dressed in white.

"Charlie told me you were looking for a friend," the woman said sternly. "Is that true?"

"His name's Ryan Daley," Vicki said.

"Are you Vicki?"

"How did you know that?"

The woman pulled a piece of paper from her pocket. "He wrote this for you."

Vicki couldn't open the letter. "I have to know if he's alive," Vicki said.

"Not for long, I'm afraid," the nurse said. "He's in a coma."

Vicki bit her lip and wiped her eyes.

"Stay a while," the nurse said.

Vicki thanked her and sat on the floor. She unfolded the letter.

> I'm writing this to you, Vicki, but I'm hoping you'll be in touch with Judd and Lionel as well.
>
> First, I shouldn't have been surprised at what happened because this was everything Bruce said. The wrath of the Lamb and all. We can be glad God keeps his promises, I guess. The nurse said I should write to you. I never was a letter writer, but she thought it was a good idea.
>
> You've been like a big sister to me. I never had one. Judd was a big brother, and Lionel was a good friend. I hope I wasn't too much of a pain to have around.
>
> I guess there's a chance I could get up and walk out of here, but it doesn't look good. So I want to tell you all to hang in there. God didn't let us survive this long without there being a reason. No matter where you go or what happens, I want

you to remember how much you mean to me. I can't thank you enough.

Maybe somebody else will come and take my place at your house or in the Young Trib Force. I hope they do. If you care for them half as much as you cared for me, they'll be really happy.

Promise me you'll take care of Phoenix. Tell Chaya and Shelly and Mark and John that I was thinking of them. I hope you all made it through the earthquake. I'll never forget you.

Love,
Ryan

Vicki lay her head on the floor and wept. *God, please don't let him die.*

THREE

Judd's Choice

VICKI sat up, clutching Ryan's note. The nurse helped her stand and took her by the shoulders to a chair in the next room.

"It's my fault," Vicki said. "I told him to stay inside! He would have been OK if I hadn't insisted—"

"Ryan was smart," the nurse said.

"Was?"

"Is," the nurse said. "You're right. There's still a chance. But either way, this is not your fault. Last night Ryan tried to tell me something but couldn't find the words."

Vicki squinted. "What did he say?"

"Something about God, but he was out of his head by then. He really got to me. He's about the same age as my son."

"Charlie?"

"No, my son disappeared in the vanishings," the nurse said.

Vicki straightened. "I know what Ryan was trying to tell you."

Tim Vetter and the other men carried bags of supplies and blankets. Judd kept his hands behind him.

"Enough provisions for a few days," Tim said. "No GC yet."

"Just leave the stuff here and I'll keep an eye on it," Marlene said.

Tim pursed his lips. "The GC has a station on the south side. We'll take him with us. You stay with the supplies."

Tim untied Judd's feet and helped him stand. Judd kept his hands tight against his back. The other men were big and burly. Tim was the only one who could catch him if Judd ran.

Judd saw his chance at the corner. With the others behind him, he took off toward a mound of earth in the center of town. Tim was a few yards behind when Judd hit the embankment.

Judd scrambled up but slipped. Tim grabbed Judd's pant leg, and the others came lumbering. Judd kicked free and struggled to the top. Tim was close behind but slipping.

The other men split into two groups, working their way around the pile.

Judd slid down the other side and raced toward a road by the river. He looked for a place to hide, but the quake had flattened houses and trees. He kept running.

"My son was a good boy," the nurse told Vicki as they walked the hallway between wards. "Never got into much trouble. Loved his video games. I was working the late shift the night it happened. It was crazy. We had pregnant women lose their unborn babies just before they were delivered. A friend of mine vanished from an operating room. It was awful.

"Then I came home to check on Chad. All that was left were his clothes. I blamed my husband at first. I guess that was wrong."

"What do you think happened?" Vicki said.

"I've read all the explanations," the nurse said. "An energy force, alien abduction, some kind of social cleansing. Whatever it was doesn't really matter. Chad's gone. When I saw Ryan, it made me think of him again."

"Did your son ever go to church?"

"As a matter of fact, he did. We went as a

family only at Christmas and Easter. But Chad got involved in a youth group with one of his friends. They met during the week for some kind of study."

Vicki took a breath. "This is going to sound weird, but I know what really happened to your son," she said. Vicki told the nurse about meeting Ryan and how Pastor Bruce Barnes had shown them a videotape that explained the vanishings. Vicki knew then that what her parents had tried to tell her had come true.

"My mom and dad tried to get me to listen," Vicki said. "They told me Jesus Christ was going to come back for his true followers. When I found their clothes, I knew I had been left behind.

"Your son was a Christian," Vicki said. "A true believer."

The nurse turned away as Charlie entered the room.

"I'm sorry that boy in there made you sad," Charlie said to Vicki.

"It's OK; he's a friend of mine," Vicki said.

The nurse gave a wary glance to Vicki and said, "I'll get in trouble if you're found in here. You need to go."

"But I want to tell you more about this," Vicki said. "And I don't want to leave Ryan."

"Come back late tonight," the nurse said.

"I'm back here around ten. I'll meet you at the back door and let you in."

"I'll bring a friend," Vicki said.

Judd doubled back on his pursuers. He crouched behind the rubble of a house while the men passed. Several others had joined the search.

"I know where some GC guards are," one of them said.

"Go find them!" Tim yelled.

When the men were a safe distance past, Judd took off. He climbed the huge mound of earth, then stopped and peered around the corner to see if Marlene was alone.

"What are you doing here?" Marlene said as Judd rushed to her.

"They'll never think of looking for me here," Judd said, out of breath.

Marlene motioned Judd to the end of the street so they could watch for the others. "You should get out of here," she said. "I don't know what they'll do to you if they catch you. But now they know something's up."

"I'm OK," Judd said. "I couldn't leave and not finish our discussion."

Marlene took a breath. "I'm interested in what you're talking about," she said, "but I can't believe like you. It's too easy. If you're right, I basically don't have to do anything."

"You got it," Judd said. "You just accept what God's done."

"I'd feel a lot better if you told me I had to do something," Marlene said.

"That's the point," Judd said. "We're help-less. That's why Jesus lived a perfect life and died for us."

Marlene stared off. "Why would God . . . ?"

"In the Bible it says God is love," Judd said. "God doesn't want anyone to die with-out knowing him. But it's up to you."

Marlene got a wild look on her face. "If what you're saying is true, that changes every-thing," she said. "The Enigma Babylon Faith is a big lie."

"Exactly," Judd said. "That's why I want you to—"

Marlene jumped back from the corner. "Here they come!"

"I'm not leaving until you—"

"You have to," she said.

"All right, but ask God to forgive you," Judd said. "Tell him you're sorry. Tell him you accept his gift."

"Go!"

"Will you do it?" Judd said.

"I'll think about it."

Judd peeked around the corner. Tim and

the others moved slowly toward them, no doubt dejected that Judd had escaped. Beside them was a GC guard.

Judd picked up the ropes he had been tied with and tied Marlene's hands and feet. He tied a rag tightly over her mouth.

"I overpowered you," Judd said. "I stole food, and you couldn't scream because I put this in your mouth. Got it?"

Marlene nodded and jerked her head, telling him to leave.

"God, thank you for letting me talk with Marlene," Judd prayed out loud. "I pray she will become your child. Keep her safe, and may she be able to tell others about you in the days ahead."

Judd heard footsteps. He ran the other way and grabbed some bread from the stash of provisions. He waited until the group turned the corner, then ducked into a brick-strewn alley.

Judd figured they had told the GC his identity, but with communication lines down, he doubted they would know he was supposed to be in a reeducation camp. They would expect him to cross the river and head toward Chicago. Instead, Judd ran the other way. Away from his home. Away from his friends.

The nurse showed Vicki the rear entrance that wasn't guarded by the GC. Vicki promised she would return late that night. "I want to talk to you more about what Ryan said," Vicki said.

"Just go," the nurse said.

Vicki circled the building and found Darrion and Shelly still waiting.

"What happened?" Shelly said.

Vicki tried to be strong, but she broke down as she told them about Ryan. Darrion took the news hard.

"What are we going to do now?" Darrion said.

"I'm coming back tonight to check on him," Vicki said.

"I'm in," Shelly said.

Darrion shook her head. "My mom. I've waited too long. I have to find her, and—"

"Don't do this," Shelly said. "The GC will be all over you. Your face has been plastered all over the news."

"I can wear a disguise," Darrion said.

"They'll lock you up like they did your mother," Shelly said.

"I don't care! She'd do the same for me. I have to find her."

Vicki led the girls back the way they came.

Shelly tried to talk Darrion out of leaving. "We need to stick together," she said. "If you leave, that's just another person we'll have to find. And if the GC gets you, you'll wind up like Judd."

Vicki looked hard at Shelly.

"Sorry," Shelly said. "I just don't want to lose anyone else."

"This is my mother," Darrion said. She looked away. "I can't expect you to understand."

"Why? Because my mom was trailer trash? Because I know she's dead?"

"I didn't mean it that way," Darrion said.

"Enough," Vicki said. "Shel, you're right, we ought to stick together. But Darrion needs to find her mom too."

"I'm really sorry about Ryan," Darrion said. "I wish I could do something to help."

Vicki said she understood. "You and Shelly should leave this afternoon and go—"

"No way," Shelly said.

"I can do this myself," Darrion said.

"I know you can," Vicki said. "That's not the point. I'll go back tonight and monitor Ryan. You've got a few hours of daylight left to find your mom. If you get into trouble, Shelly can help."

Darrion frowned and looked at Shelly. "I didn't mean to knock your mom."

Shelly looked away.

"Would you come with me?"

"I think it's the best idea, Shel," Vicki said.

Shelly sighed. "I guess if that's what Vick thinks I should do."

"We're almost to the end of the expressway," Darrion said. "The GC holding place was a few miles from here."

"I know where it is," Shelly said. "There's no way we can make it there and back before nightfall."

"Find a shelter nearby and stay till morning," Vicki said. "I'll meet you back at the tent tomorrow afternoon."

"Wait," Shelly said. "How are you going to get to Ryan after curfew? If you're out, you'll get shot."

"I've got a plan," Vicki said.

Judd ran south along the interstate, backtracking until he came to the bridge where he had helped the motorcycle rider, Pete. He hopped on the back of a four-wheel drive pickup that was transporting more bodies to the morgue.

When they arrived, Judd was surprised to see the injured lying outside on the ground.

"Did they spend the night out here?" Judd asked a volunteer.

"The nearest hospital's flat," the man said. "Other buildings aren't safe. You got a better idea?"

Judd located a list of injured and looked for Pete's name. He was afraid the man had died but was relieved when he flipped the page over. Pete's name was on the back.

Judd didn't want to upset the man, but he knew he had to tell him the bad news about Pete's girlfriend. Judd found him sitting up and groggy.

"Didn't expect to see you for a long time," Pete said. "Couldn't make it to Chicago?"

"Ran into a little problem and had to leave your bike at the bottom of the river; sorry, man. How are you?"

"Doc says I have some temporary nerve damage," Pete said. "I feel pretty tingly right now, but I'm OK. It'll take more than that to do me in. You find my place?"

"Yeah," Judd said. "You left your bike outside the shed. It was a good thing, because everything else was destroyed."

Pete grimaced. "Same for the house?"

"I'm afraid so," Judd said.

Judd knelt beside the big man. The day before Judd had explained the forgiveness offered in Christ, and Pete had prayed. Pete's one concern was that his girlfriend hear what Judd had said.

"I managed to get inside the house," Judd said. "I couldn't find your friend for a long time and thought she might have gotten out. Then . . ."

"Oh, no," Pete said.

"She was in the laundry room when the quake hit. She didn't suffer."

Pete shook his head and wept. Judd felt embarrassed seeing such a big man cry. Judd put his hand on Pete's shoulder.

"What you said yesterday changed me," Pete said. "It really did. All I could think about was telling Rosie. Now she's gone."

Night fell. Pete cried. Judd slept on the ground beside him.

FOUR

Ryan's Friend

VICKI waited until dark, then made her way
back to the hospital. She encountered Global
Community guards and police several times.
She dropped to the ground and waited until
they passed.

Vicki crouched low when she came near
the furniture store. Huge spotlights lit the
receiving area. Vicki stole to the back and
waited for the nurse. There was no way she
was getting inside the front of the building
with what she had planned. Finally, the back
door opened.

"You have to come quickly," the nurse
said.

"Is Ryan still alive?"

"Yes. Barely."

"You go ahead," Vicki said. "I don't want
to get you in trouble."

The nurse left the door ajar. Vicki moved
into the shadows, grabbed Phoenix's collar,

and walked him inside. The dog panted and followed obediently.

"You have to be really quiet," Vicki said, hoping Phoenix would understand.

Vicki led Phoenix up the back stairs to the third floor. She reached for the door but heard footsteps and scampered back down the steps. A GC guard opened the door. The beam of the flashlight narrowly missed her. After a few moments, the man closed the door and walked away. Vicki headed for Ryan's room.

Phoenix shook, as if he were scared of the makeshift hospital. The strong medicine smell and all the bodies seemed to spook him. When he reached Ryan's side, the dog sniffed at the boy and licked his hand.

"I brought your best friend," Vicki whispered in Ryan's ear.

Phoenix put his paws on the bed and licked Ryan's face.

"What in the world?" the nurse said as she walked into the room. "Get that animal out of here! I could lose my job!"

"You don't understand," Vicki pleaded. "This is his best friend. They've been together—"

Vicki stopped when she saw the look on the nurse's face. The nurse pointed to the bed.

Ryan's hand twitched, and his eyes fluttered. Vicki's heart raced as she watched.

"Ryan, it's me, Vicki!"

Ryan tried to open his eyes but couldn't.

"It's OK," Vicki said. "I'll do the talking."

Vicki told Ryan where he was and that he had been hurt in the earthquake. Ryan nodded, and with each sentence he seemed to stir a little more.

Phoenix wagged his tail and whimpered.

"Lamb," Ryan finally said.

"That's right," Vicki said, "the wrath of the Lamb!"

"Water," Ryan said with a raspy voice.

Vicki grabbed a plastic pitcher and poured him a glass. Ryan's lips were chapped. She put the cup to his lips and helped him drink slowly.

"How did you find me?" Ryan said.

Vicki wiped away a tear. She was so overjoyed to talk with Ryan she choked as she spoke. "I had some help," was all she could say.

"What about the others?"

"Darrion and Shelly are OK. Judd was still in GC custody when the quake hit."

"Lionel?"

"Haven't heard," Vicki said.

Ryan looked toward his nightstand. "The letter."

"I got it," Vicki said. "Now listen to me. You're going to be OK. You'll pull out of this."

"No," Ryan said. He reached out and weakly patted Phoenix on the head. The dog licked him. Ryan's hand fell to the bed. "I'm ready."

"I know you are," Vicki said. "You have to get better; then we'll get you out of here."

Ryan shook his head. "Going home."

Vicki took his hand. "I can't move you right now or I would, you know that," she said.

Ryan smiled. "You don't get it."

"What don't I get?"

Ryan tried to raise his arm. He pointed a finger to the ceiling. Vicki bent closer as he said, "Home in heaven."

Vicki felt a chill go through her. "No. You've been through a lot, but you're still here. There's a lot the doctors can do."

He tried to sit up but couldn't. "When I went to the hospital the day of the bombings, Bruce couldn't talk much," Ryan said. "I think he knew he was going to die."

"That was different. We've lost too much as it is. You can't go."

"Friends," Ryan said. "They're waiting. I want to see Bruce. Raymie. Mrs. Steele."

"You'll get to see them soon enough," Vicki said. "You have to hang on."

The nurse touched Vicki's shoulder. "Can I talk to you a minute?" she said.

"I'll be right back," Vicki said to Ryan.

"As a nurse, you see things," the woman whispered. "I think he hung on because he thought you'd come. He's doing this for you."

"Then why won't he fight it?" Vicki said. "He can't die. I won't let him."

"It's not your fight," the nurse said. "You talked about believing in God. You must think Ryan's going to a better place."

"Yes, but not now. Not yet."

The nurse took Vicki's face in her hands. "He needs you to be strong. He needs you to tell him you'll be OK."

Vicki wiped her tears and nodded. "I just don't know if I will be."

Vicki returned to Ryan. His eyes were closed, his face pale. His hair was a mess. White beads formed at the corner of his mouth. Suddenly, Ryan's eyes fluttered. His face flushed with color. He smiled.

"They're coming," Ryan said.

"Who's coming?" Vicki said. "Who is it?"

Ryan opened his eyes and stared at Vicki. "I have to go now," he said. "I'm sorry."

Vicki wanted to scream. She wanted to run from the room. But she knew God had allowed her to be with Ryan in the final moments of his life. She had to think of Ryan, not herself. But it was so hard. She couldn't imagine what life would be like without him.

"I'll be OK," Vicki said.

"You have to stay safe," Ryan said. "Who will take care of Phoenix?"

Vicki smiled. "Hey, I was the one who talked Judd into letting you keep him."

Ryan closed his eyes again. "Can you hear them?" he said.

"Who?" Vicki said, but Ryan didn't answer.

Vicki buried her head in her hands. She and Ryan had been through so many scrapes together.

The nurse touched her shoulder. "It's time," she said.

Vicki summoned all her strength and took her friend's hand. "Ryan," she whispered, "you've been like a little brother to me. And you've been so brave."

Ryan smiled. A tear escaped one eye and rolled the length of his cheek.

"You have to trust me on this, OK?"

Ryan squeezed her hand.

"I don't want you to go. I want you to live

and see the Glorious Appearing of Jesus like Bruce talked about. But if you have to go now, I understand. It won't be the same without you."

Vicki turned and wiped her eyes.

"I feel like I'm letting you down," Ryan said.

"No," Vicki said, "don't ever think that. You've never let me down."

"You'll be OK?" Ryan said.

"Yeah. But you have to do me a favor."

"Anything."

Vicki closed her eyes and put her head next to Ryan's. "When you get home, will you tell Bruce I said hello?"

Ryan raised his head a few inches and opened his eyes. He looked straight at Vicki. "I'll tell him you were the best big sister anybody ever had."

He smiled again, then rested his head on the pillow and closed his eyes.

"So don't worry, OK?" Vicki said. "I'll take care of Phoenix. He'll take care of me."

A few minutes passed. Vicki watched as Ryan faded. His breathing became erratic. Phoenix whimpered.

Vicki came close to Ryan and whispered in his ear, "I love you."

"Love you," Ryan whispered.

Then his chest fell with a final breath, and he was gone.

Judd heard someone scream and awoke. Pete thrashed about yelling his girlfriend's name. Judd subdued the big man.

"Too late," the man cried. "We were too late to save Rosie."

"Just hold still," Judd said. Then he realized the man was moving his lower body.

"Pete," Judd said, "your legs!"

Pete looked startled, then gingerly sat up. "Help me," he said.

Judd helped him stand, wobbly at first, then Pete stood straight. "Look at me," he said. "Bet you didn't know I was this tall."

In a few minutes, Pete was walking. A few patients roused and clapped softly.

"You've got a little limp," Judd said.

"I'll take it," Pete said. "Come on, let's get out of here."

"You can't just walk away," Judd said.

"Watch me," Pete said. "I have work to do."

Vicki sat with Ryan a few minutes longer. The nurse felt for his pulse, then said, "He's gone." She knelt in front of Vicki and put a hand on her shoulder.

"You did a good thing here today. You made his last moments easier. I'm glad you came."

Vicki cried. She felt an emptiness she'd never felt before. When she lost her parents and family, she hadn't been able to say good-bye. She woke up the next morning, and they were gone. But this was different. Ryan's body was right next to her. She knew he wasn't there any longer, and her heart ached.

"What happens now?" Vicki said.

"With so many bodies, they aren't doing many burials. A lot of them are being burned."

"I don't want that for him."

"There's no way around it."

"Can you give me a few hours?" Vicki said. "I could find someone to help me carry him."

"It's out of the question. As soon as I report him deceased, they'll take him away."

"Can't you hold off till morning?" Vicki said.

"I don't know—"

"Please," Vicki said.

"I can try," the nurse said.

Phoenix jumped onto Ryan's bed and whimpered.

"Get down!" the nurse said.

Phoenix barked. A few patients stirred.

"You have to get him out of here!"

Phoenix barked again. Vicki grabbed him by the collar and headed for the stairs. She heard someone running up and looked through the window.

"GC guard!" Vicki said.

"In here!"

Vicki ducked into a closet with Phoenix as the door to the stairwell opened. Phoenix panted. Vicki clamped his mouth shut. She heard the muffled sounds of the guard and the nurse.

"I heard a dog bark," the guard said.

"Up here?" the nurse said. "You've gotta be kidding."

Another bark. Phoenix perked up his ears.

The guard shouted something. A door closed. A moment later, the nurse ushered Vicki and Phoenix out. Charlie was standing by the exit sign.

"I got chewed out, chewed out good," Charlie said with a grin. "I was watchin' you guys. Hope that was OK."

The nurse frowned. "I have to go on rounds. Get out fast before they find you."

"Yes, ma'am," Vicki said.

"I can do really good dog sounds," Charlie said. "I saw the guy come looking for your dog, so I made it sound like him, and the guy thought I was the dog. Pretty neat, huh?"

"Yeah," Vicki said, heading for the door.

"I can do a squirrel too. You wanna hear?"

"Not right now," Vicki said.

Charlie came close and whispered, "I can help you."

"You can help me do what?"

"Carry your friend," Charlie said. "I'm a real good carrier. One time I helped my sister carry a piano all the way from her apartment—"

"You want to help me carry Ryan?"

"Carry Ryan," Charlie repeated. "Carry him anywhere you want. Actually, I didn't carry the piano from her apartment, I dragged it—"

"OK," Vicki said, "I'd like your help, but we have to hurry."

Pete led Judd out of the camp. They found a man asleep in his truck, and Pete convinced him to give them a ride. A few minutes later, Judd and Pete were in front of Pete's demolished house.

"We should wait until morning," Judd said.

"I can't let her stay in there another minute," Pete said.

Pete found an old lantern, and the two tore wood from the house until they reached

Rosie's body. The sun was nearly up when Pete carefully carried her from the rubble. He dug a grave by the creek that passed his property and gently placed her in the ground.

"I don't know what to say," Pete said. "Shouldn't we read something or pray?"

"Whatever's in your heart," Judd said.

Pete sighed and bowed his head. He looked like a mountain. "God, I don't think Rosie knew about you. I'd give anything to talk to her now.

"I know I don't deserve you forgiving me after all I've done, but I believe you have. Help me to live right and follow you and make you proud. Thank you for my new friend. Amen."

Pete looked at Judd. "How was that?"

"Straight from the heart," Judd said. "You can't get better than that."

Pete threw his shovel at the demolished shed. "Now we gotta get you back to Chicago."

Vicki led Phoenix out. Charlie carried Ryan's lifeless body. As they slipped into the night, Charlie huffed and puffed. Vicki could tell it wasn't going to be an easy trip. They rested as often as Charlie needed. At times, Vicki helped, but mostly Charlie carried Ryan alone.

A flood of memories came over her as they walked. Ryan had grown taller since they first met. She remembered their trips searching for Bibles. She had been there when Ryan found Phoenix. She had seen Ryan stand at Bruce's memorial service and say he was willing to give his life for the sake of the gospel.

By morning, they were near Vicki's house. Construction crews were busy clearing rubble and collapsed roadways. Vicki took Charlie near the spot where New Hope Village Church once stood.

While Charlie scampered off to find a shovel, Vicki pawed through the loose stones that led to Ryan's secret chamber. There was no sign of life at the church. Vicki moved enough dirt and bricks to crawl through. She grabbed a Bible and crawled out.

When Charlie was finished digging the grave, Vicki helped him lift Ryan. She unfolded the sheet from around him and placed the Bible in his hands.

"Is that for luck?" Charlie said.

"No," Vicki said. "The Bible was really important to him. He studied it just about every day."

"I had a Bible once," Charlie said. "Somebody took it."

Vicki reached into the grave and took the book from Ryan's body.

"What are you doing?" Charlie said.

"He wouldn't have wanted to be buried with it," Vicki said. "He'd want you to have it."

As the sun rose, Vicki knelt on the cold ground. She looked at Ryan, and the tears came. Charlie stood back, his head bowed.

Softly, Vicki sang the words to one of Ryan's favorite hymns.

> *Amazing grace! how sweet the sound—*
> *That saved a wretch like me!*
> *I once was lost but now am found,*
> *Was blind but now I see.*

She made a crude cross and stuck it in the ground at the head of the grave. She wondered how many more crosses she would have to make in the days ahead.

FIVE

Commander Blancka

Vicki awoke near Ryan's grave. Phoenix was sprawled out on top. When Vicki moved, Phoenix whimpered and pawed at the loose dirt. Charlie was gone.

Vicki shivered from the cold. She wished she could see Judd and talk with him about Ryan. If this was what it would be like for the rest of the Tribulation, she didn't know if she could go on.

God, why did you have to take him? Vicki prayed.

Vicki returned to the shelter but couldn't find Shelly or Darrion. A man asked for volunteers. "We need help with the injured."

Vicki raised a hand and followed him.

Lionel took the gun instructions seriously. He watched carefully as the instructor taught them how to clean it and use it safely. At the

51

shooting range Lionel scored the highest. The instructor patted him on the shoulder. "Watch this guy and you'll learn how to shoot," the man told a girl beside Lionel.

"I'm not that good," Lionel said when the instructor left.

"Better than me," the girl said. She held out a hand. "I'm Felicia."

Lionel introduced himself, then headed to the morning session. "Once you've blended in with the communities you'll be sent to," the instructor said, "you'll listen for specific things. No one in their right mind is going to come out and say they're against the Global Community."

A computer generated images and phrases on a screen in front of the class. The words *Antichrist* and *Tribulation* flashed before Lionel.

"Anyone who talks about there being an Antichrist is someone you want to watch closely. If the person believes we are experiencing what they call the 'Tribulation,' these may be enemies of the Global Community."

The instructor stopped and looked over his glasses. "There are actually people who believe Nicolae Carpathia is an evil man." The class responded with groans and laughter.

A Global Community chopper landed in a

nearby field, interrupting the class. The sound of the rotor blades was deafening.

"You are witnessing the arrival of your new boss," the instructor said. "Terrel Blancka. Never—I repeat—never call him by his first name. You'll want to call him Commander Blancka or simply Commander."

Lionel watched as a man with a barrel chest and a graying mustache strode to the practice area. He wore a GC field uniform with a beret. He carried a clipboard and spoke gruffly to the instructor.

"What do you make of him?" Conrad asked Lionel.

"Looks like he means business," Lionel whispered.

The instructor formally introduced Commander Blancka, and the burly man stood ramrod straight, his hands behind his back.

"Boys and girls," Commander Blancka said, "and you are boys and girls until we get through with you." He scanned the group for any response. When there was none, he continued. "I've made it no secret that I didn't want this assignment. I don't have time to baby-sit. But when the most powerful man in the world calls and gives an order, I follow it.

"Now listen carefully. You are part of an elite group, chosen for a specific purpose. You are the first of the Global Community's Morale Monitors.

"There's no question you're young. But that doesn't have to be a drawback. We think it's an asset. We'll send you into hot spots, places where we feel there may be resistance to the purposes of the Global Community. I can't emphasize enough the importance of this job. Let me tell you about my conversation with the potentate."

Lionel caught a glance from Conrad. Commander Blancka's message made Lionel feel important.

"Nicolae Carpathia came to me and asked that I put this program together," the commander continued. "The success or failure of it depends on you. And that means my success or failure depends on you. So I'll be watching."

Commander Blancka looked steely eyed at the crowd. "That means you will succeed. The potentate made it clear. The secret to the success of the Global Community is UNITY!" The kids jumped as the commander shouted.

"Those who want to divide us will be exposed. People who want to live in peace and harmony will enjoy exactly that. But those who want to cause trouble will be dealt with. Swiftly."

A boy near Conrad timidly raised a hand.

"What!" Commander Blancka barked.

"Is the potentate safe, sir?" the boy said.

"Good question," Commander Blancka said. "Nicolae Carpathia was prepared for this. He's in a safe place, getting ready to have his ten international ambassadors join him. Any more questions?"

Felicia raised a hand. "Sir, from what you've said, we're in kind of a war, aren't we?"

"You bet we are," Commander Blancka said. "But not with bombs and artillery. We're in a war of thought. We can enforce laws on people's actions, but we want to go beyond that. The potentate said he wanted a group of elite enforcers of pure thought. Healthy young men and women like yourselves. Strong people who are devoted to the cause of the Global Community. So devoted that they would be willing to train and build themselves. We want people eager to make sure everyone is in line with the potentate."

The commander scanned the crowd. It seemed to Lionel that the man looked in each person's eyes. "Are you that group?" he said.

"Yes, sir," the kids said.

"You call that eager?" Commander Blancka barked.

"Yes, sir!" the kids said louder.

"That's better," Commander Blancka said. "You will not wear uniforms. We want you to blend in with the rest of society. You will, at all times, carry your weapon and a communication device. If you find yourself in mortal danger, or if you discover a situation to report, contact the base immediately. The communicator also works as a homing device so we can find you if we need to.

"One of the hallmarks of the society you've grown up in is free speech." Commander Blancka bowed his head and shook it. "Sadly, we can't afford that luxury. That's why we've trained you. You will root out those who by word or action oppose the purposes of our cause.

"A good soldier knows his or her enemy," the commander said, pacing now. "Who is the enemy? If you're smart, you're asking that question. I'll tell you. The enemy is anyone who seeks to divide. Anyone who says *they* know what's right and not the potentate. One of our main targets will be those fundamentalists who say their religion is the only true religion."

Lionel raised a hand. "What power are we given, sir?" he said.

"A Global Community Morale Monitor has no limit to his or her powers," the commander said. "We find the enemy. We subdue the enemy. By any means necessary."

"That means using a gun?" Lionel said.

"That means using whatever we must. If you do your job well, we'll have no need for you within a few years. The enemy will vanish."

After a few hours of sleep, Judd and Pete set out to locate another motorcycle. They found a large one at Pete's friend's house. The man had also been killed by the earthquake. Before they left, Judd located an old laptop computer in an office near the front of the house.

"I could use this to make contact with some friends," Judd said. "You think we can take it?"

"My friend's not gonna use it anymore," Pete said.

Pete showed Judd another route home. "You'll want to avoid the place you just came from."

"Actually, I'd like to go back the other way."

"You've gotta be outta your mind!" Pete said.

Judd explained the situation with Marlene. "I have to know if she accepted Christ."

"Don't you think that's too dangerous?" Pete said. "People have to make their own decisions."

"True. But I have to know."

"Then you won't go alone," Pete said.

"What do you mean?"

"We'll get close enough; then you point her out to me. I'll see if I can talk to her."

Judd smiled and nodded. He noticed a bruise on Pete's forehead. "I didn't see this the other day," Judd said.

"Must have smacked my head when they were transporting me," Pete said. "Besides, you've got a smudge of your own."

Judd looked in the mirror but didn't see anything.

Lionel paid attention as Commander Blancka warned the kids. "We don't know about radiation with the meteors," he said. "Best to stay away from them. Avoid looking like an authority. Blend in. Make friends. But always remember you have the power to enforce the Global Community's rules."

"Do we go back to school?" a girl asked.

"School as you knew it, no. The Global

Community has an education plan for the future. Central learning stations are being built as we speak. GC-approved instructors will teach via satellite links from New Babylon. You'll uplink for tests and research. Everyone will be required to participate."

When Commander Blancka completed his speech, he told the kids to be ready to leave the following morning. "You Monitors will be airlifted by helicopter."

"Why do they have someone that high up in charge of us?" Conrad asked after the meeting was over.

"You heard him," Lionel said. "What we're doing's important."

"But we're kids," Conrad said.

"We're GCMM now," Lionel said. "Get used to it."

Conrad pulled out his gun and twirled it on his finger. Lionel grabbed it angrily. "You know that's dangerous!"

Conrad took his gun and holstered it. "It's not loaded," he said. "Besides, who died and left you in charge?"

Lionel stared at Conrad. "If you don't think this is serious, why don't you quit?" he said.

"So, your first job is to monitor the Morale Monitors?"

"If I have to," Lionel said.

Conrad walked away.

Vicki helped in the main tent. The suffering was unbelievable. Finally she spotted Darrion and Shelly. She excused herself and caught up with them. Shelly looked exhausted. Darrion sat with elbows on knees. She didn't look up when Vicki ran to them.

"What happened?" Vicki said.

Shelly shook her head. "Long story. Bad ending."

"Mom's gone," Darrion said. "They had her locked in a cell. After all this time they were still questioning her."

"They wouldn't show us the facility," Shelly said. "It was roped off and patrolled. We stayed till dark to get a look."

"There's no way she could have survived," Darrion said. "The place was knocked flat. The whole thing must have come down on her."

"I'm sorry," Vicki said.

"We did get a look at the logbook," Shelly said. "Judd and Taylor Graham were taken away on the morning of the quake."

"So there's a chance they're still alive," Vicki said.

Shelly nodded. Vicki noticed something strange on Shelly's forehead. Shelly rubbed at the smudge, but it didn't come off. "What's it look like?" Shelly said.

"Like what they do in Catholic churches around Ash Wednesday," Vicki said.

"Maybe I tripped or something," Shelly said. "It was a long night. What about Ryan?"

Vicki told them. Darrion hung her head. Shelly lay back on the ground. "I can't even cry anymore," she said.

Vicki took them to the grave. Phoenix hadn't moved. The three girls stood in silence. Vicki wondered about Lionel. And Judd.

Judd described Marlene and told Pete where he might find the group. Pete dropped Judd off at a gas station that was still standing.

"I'll wait for you here," Judd said, taking the laptop with him.

The service station owner sat in a lawn chair near the gas pumps and held a large dog by the collar. The dog lunged at Judd. Judd saw the butt of a gun sticking out of the man's belt.

"You best move on," the man said, spitting in the dirt. "All the food's gone."

"Can I use your rest room? My friend will be back for me soon."

The man nodded to the corner of the building.

Judd noticed a telephone behind the counter when he returned. A light blinked on one of its lines.

"Is that phone working?" Judd asked.

"They're tryin'," the man said. "Comes and goes."

"Would you mind if I tried to hook up my computer?" Judd said.

"It'll cost you."

Judd had no wallet. No identification. The Global Community had taken all he had. He had scrounged for food since the earthquake. He wondered how he would live without money.

The man rolled his eyes when he saw Judd pat his pockets. "Local call?" the man said.

"Yeah," Judd said, "I just need to get the access number."

"I don't understand those things. Go ahead and use it if you have to."

Judd tried several times to dial out but got a busy signal each time. On the fifth try he got a ring and located the number for a dial-up line.

The computer was old and slow, but Judd felt like he was holding a gold mine. It was his first cyber contact with the outside world since he'd been arrested.

Judd first downloaded his messages but saw none from Vicki, Lionel, or Ryan. Next, he located a Web site with a people search. The Global Community was already tracking the number of deaths. He entered Vicki Byrne's name and held his breath. The computer ground slowly, then showed Vicki in the "no known whereabouts" listing.

At least she's not confirmed dead, Judd thought.

Judd entered Lionel Washington's name. "Injured." Judd typed in Ryan's name. "Confirmed dead."

Judd gasped. Could it be true? Could Ryan really be dead?

He typed in his own name. "No known whereabouts."

He checked the adult Tribulation Force. Rayford Steele was "confirmed alive." Chloe and Buck Williams were not accounted for. The same for Loretta and Donny Moore.

When Judd typed in Amanda Steele's name, he again gasped as he read, "Subject confirmed on Boston to New Babylon nonstop, reported crashed and submerged in Tigris River, no survivors."

Judd figured Amanda had been flying to see Rayford in New Babylon. The report said she hadn't made it. Judd hung his head. When would the death toll stop?

Judd called up his E-mail again and looked at the multiple lines of messages. He heard a click of the modem and realized the phone was dead. One message interested him. It was from Pavel, the boy from New Babylon he had met online. He tried to dial up again, but the line was dead. Judd wondered if Pavel had made it through the earthquake. If it was the worldwide quake the Bible talked about, being outside when it hit was probably the boy's only chance.

Judd tried to dial up again but couldn't get through. He heard a loud rumbling and saw at least ten motorcycles pull into the gas station. The dog barked, and the owner reached for his gun.

"No!" Judd shouted.

SIX

The Mark

JUDD's shout startled the owner and the riders. The group turned and stared at Judd as he ran toward them.

"Don't do this," Judd said.

"Stay out of it, kid," the biker nearest the owner said. He was huge and had long red hair.

"They think they're comin' in here and stealin' my gas," the owner said. "Over my dead body."

"Whatever it takes," the biker snorted.

The dog barked wildly as the hairy man got off his bike and approached the owner.

"I'm warnin' you," the owner said.

Judd heard another cycle. A trail of dust lifted in the distance. A moment later, Judd saw Pete flying along the path he had taken toward town.

"Is that who I think it is?" a girl on the back of one bike said.

"Sure looks like him," the hairy man said.

Pete took his time climbing off the cycle. Even the dog stopped barking. Pete pulled off his helmet and ambled toward the others.

"Pete?" the hairy man said.

"What's up, Red?"

"Just looking for a little gas, that's all."

Pete stopped in front of the owner and pawed at the ground with his boot. "This looks like an honest businessman," Pete said.

"Cash only," the owner said.

"Don't do this," Red said to Pete. "You get in our way, and there'll be trouble."

Pete stepped nose to nose with Red. Their combined weight was surely more than 600 pounds.

"I'm trying to keep you from doing something you'll regret," Pete said. "Now pay the man or leave."

Red clenched his teeth and his fists. Finally he turned and waved a hand. "Come on. We'll fuel up later."

As the dust settled from Red's gang's departure, the owner turned to Pete. "Sure am glad you two came along," he said, giving a toothless smile. "Fill your tank. It's on me."

"It was nothing," Pete said. "But get ready. I don't think you've seen the last of them."

"Did you find her?" Judd said.

Pete nodded, then asked the owner, "Mind if we use your office to talk?"

"Go right ahead," the owner said.

"I found the people," Pete said when they were a safe distance away. "Told them I was looking for a skinny kid who stole my motorcycle."

"Thanks a lot!" Judd said.

"They're still looking for you. Said you took some stuff and ran from the GC."

"I was hungry," Judd said. "I took a few pieces of bread. Give me a break."

"I saw the little lady you talked about."

"Talk with her?"

"Couldn't," Pete said, moving closer. Pete was only a few inches away. "But I saw the weirdest thing."

Judd stepped back. "What's the matter with you?"

"She's got the same kind of smudge on her forehead that you do."

Judd found a broken mirror in the bathroom but couldn't see the smudge. "Let me see your head again."

Pete leaned forward in the light and pulled back his long hair. Judd studied the mark closely. "This isn't a bruise like I thought," he said. "It's some kind of stamp or a mark.

Maybe they put it on you at the shelter to keep track of patients."

"I don't remember it if they did," Pete said.

"It's almost like one of those 3-D images."

"You're right," Pete said, looking at Judd. "Holy cow, it looks like a cross."

"You see that on my forehead?" Judd said, looking in the mirror again.

"Yeah. I can see yours and you can see mine, but not in a mirror. What do you think it is?"

Judd's mind raced. "The pastor I told you about, Bruce Barnes, taught about a mark people would have, but that was supposed to be given by the Antichrist. People will have to take it in order to buy and sell stuff."

Pete threw up his hands. "Hey, don't look at me. I'm new to this."

Judd ran to the computer and tried the dial-up. This time he got through and went straight to Tsion Ben-Judah's Web site.

"And Marlene had this same thing on her head?" Judd asked.

"Plain as day," Pete said.

Judd did a search of Tsion's Web site. "Bingo," Judd said. Pete looked over his shoulder as Judd read, " 'Many of you have noticed a mysterious mark the size of a thumbprint on the forehead of other believers. Do not be alarmed. This is the seal, visible only to other believers.' "

"A seal?"

"Yeah, like a stamp of approval," Judd said.

"And other people don't see it?"

"Go try it out," Judd said.

Pete walked outside to the owner. Pete pulled back his hair and said, "You see anything on my forehead?"

"Some lines and hair is all I see," the owner said. "Is there supposed to be something up there?"

"I guess not," Pete said. He came back to Judd, shaking his head. "This Bible stuff is gettin' weird."

"Listen to this," Judd said. " 'The seventh chapter of Revelation tells of "the servants of our God" being sealed on their foreheads.' "

"Why would God do that?"

"I don't know. I'm just glad he did. Now we know Marlene is a true believer. She has the mark. She must have prayed after I left."

"I wonder if it'll help us in the future," Pete said.

"How?"

"I assume it'll be good to know who's on our side and who's not," Pete said.

Vicki collapsed in her tent. She had been working nonstop for hours. The number of injured and dead was staggering. Men and women walked in a daze looking for friends and family. Grown men thrashed about, saying they wanted to die.

Vicki was almost asleep when Shelly opened the tent. "There's a man out here to see you."

"Who is it?" Vicki said.

"I don't know, but I told him you were taking a rest. He said I should come wake you."

Vicki gasped when she saw the man. Chaya's father, Mr. Stein, stood a few yards from the tent.

"Vicki," Mr. Stein said.

Vicki rushed to him. "I haven't seen Chaya. She went to your house to—"

Mr. Stein held up a hand. "I was with her at the house. I made a solemn vow to find her friends. I'm here to keep that promise."

"What happened?"

"Chaya is dead," Mr. Stein said.

Vicki fell to her knees. "No," she choked.

Mr. Stein knelt beside Vicki. "We were in the house together when the earthquake hit," he said. "We were trapped many hours. If they had found us earlier, she might still be alive."

Vicki closed her eyes. "I'm so sorry."

"I have lost everything. My wife. My daughter. My home and all my possessions." Mr. Stein looked away. "But what good are possessions when the people you love are gone?"

"Were you able to talk with her before. . . ."

"You know I did not want to speak with her again," Mr. Stein said. "We had great differences. But in those hours, I understood how wrong I was."

"Wrong about what?"

"For shutting her out. She was my flesh and blood."

"Did you talk?"

Mr. Stein nodded. "She tried to convince me that her belief in God was right and mine was wrong. Until the very end she was talking about her belief in Jesus as Messiah."

"She prayed for you constantly," Vicki said.

"She was misguided."

"A funeral. Would it be all right with you if—"

"There is no need," Mr. Stein said. "I buried her yesterday."

Vicki felt crushed. Ryan. Mrs. Stahley. Donny Moore. All dead. And now Chaya, the person who had the best grasp of the Bible of any in the Young Tribulation Force.

"Why, God?" Vicki whispered.

"I thought you had it figured out. Your God was supposed to have a plan. He wants good things to happen, right?"

Vicki shook her head. "Mr. Stein, whether you believe it or not, your daughter loved you. And God loves you. He wants you to know him not just by rules and laws, but—"

Mr. Stein put up a hand. "I did not come for another sermon. I made a promise to find you, and I kept my word."

Mr. Stein turned to leave.

"The Bible doesn't say God will only cause good things to happen," Vicki said. "It says he takes everything that happens and works it for good to those who love him."

Mr. Stein frowned. "I am through arguing."

Vicki put her face in her hands.

"Do you have need of anything?" Mr. Stein said.

"We're like everyone else now. No house. No food. We'll make it somehow."

Mr. Stein handed her a card. "I don't know when the phone lines will return, but if you have need, call me or come see me. My office escaped serious damage. I may be able to help you in some way."

Lionel and Conrad packed for their trip north. The group waited near two choppers where Commander Blancka and his staff would transport them. Lionel knew he and Conrad would be in the Chicago area, along with Felicia and another girl, Melinda.

"How do they expect us to cover an area that big with four people?" Conrad said.

"Remember," Lionel said, "they're testing the program. If it works, they'll expand it."

"I've heard there's a lot of looting in Chicago," Conrad said. "Think we'll get mixed up in that?"

"I talked with the instructor after the commander left. He said we aren't peace officers, but in an emergency, you never know."

Conrad pulled a sheet of paper from his pocket. "I found that rabbi guy's Web site on the Internet."

"So?"

Conrad pointed to a paragraph at the bottom of the page. "This caught my eye. It says the good people are supposed to have some kind of a mark on their forehead."

Lionel smirked. "Why are you wasting your time on this? I don't see any mark on your forehead; do you see one on mine?"

"Guess not," Conrad said.

Lionel crumpled the paper and threw it away. "Get some sleep tonight. We've got a long flight tomorrow."

Conrad left. Lionel tried to sleep but couldn't. He went into the bathroom and looked in the mirror. There was no mark.

Judd finally opened his E-mail and checked the message from Pavel. The boy had miraculously survived the wrath of the Lamb earthquake along with a nurse who was attending him.

"The nurse insisted we go outside," Pavel wrote. "Animals were going crazy. Then the earth started shaking. We were near the main building where Nicolae has his office. After a few moments, it crashed to the ground."

Pavel asked Judd to write if he had survived. Judd logged on and sent a message to see if Pavel might be online. In a moment, Judd heard a ding and saw Pavel's response.

"I'm so glad to know you're OK," Pavel wrote. "Shall we put on the video link?"

"Stay with text, I'm on an old machine," Judd wrote. Judd briefly explained what had happened to him and how he was trying to get back to Chicago. "What about Carpathia?" Judd wrote.

"Alive and well," Pavel wrote.

"Any news on his pilot? His name is Rayford Steele."

"Haven't heard, but if the rabbi is right, your friend should be safe. Tsion Ben-Judah believes the Scriptures say the Antichrist will stay alive until a little over a year from now. If the pilot is close to Carpathia, it may be the safest place."

"What about your father?"

"He's OK. And he tells the strangest story about Nicolae. Carpathia escaped certain death when he took a helicopter from the roof of his office. But his right-hand man didn't make it."

"Leon Fortunato?"

"Exactly. How did you know?"

"I met him once," Judd typed, smiling.

"My father said Fortunato is telling the story everywhere that Nicolae raised him from the dead!"

"That can't be!"

"My father was in Nicolae's shelter. It's a huge underground facility big enough for Nicolae's airplanes. Suddenly, the potentate walks in with Fortunato. Leon was covered with dirt."

"That doesn't prove anything."

"Fortunato tells it like it is fact," Pavel wrote. "He told the staff he fell to the bottom of the building, struck his head, and died. The next thing he remembers, he hears Nicolae's voice saying, 'Leonardo, come forth.' "

A chill went down Judd's spine. "Those are the same words Jesus used to call Lazarus from the grave. Sounds like a counterfeit to me."

"I know from reading different passages that a person dies once," Pavel wrote. "There are no second chances. But still, Fortunato lives."

"There has to be an explanation."

"I'm afraid people will be fooled," Pavel said. "The potentate will soon broadcast live to the world."

"I'm not in a place where I can see or hear anything from the media."

"I'll send you the text of his message once it is complete. My greatest fear is that people will proclaim Nicolae divine."

"Let's pray it doesn't happen," Judd said.

Judd heard the rumble of motorcycles and signed off. "Hopefully, I'll write you from Chicago."

Pete moved to the front window. "They're back."

"Maybe we should get out of here," Judd said.

"And let that old man fend for himself? I know how these people operate. They're like wolves. The old guy'll be so scared he won't be able to shoot anything. I'm not leaving him alone."

"How do you know so much about these people?"

"I used to be one of them."

SEVEN

The New Pete

THE OWNER of the gas station darted inside and shut off the gas pumps. Pete brought his bike inside and closed the garage doors. "Put your laptop away," Pete said as he went out the door. "We might have to get out fast."

"What's he gonna do?" the owner asked Judd.

"You got me," Judd said.

The gang pulled in and circled around Pete. The group had grown to twenty bikes. Judd couldn't hear what they were saying, but Red shouted, and Pete stood his ground.

The owner pulled his gun, and Judd put out his hand. "A little fuel isn't worth getting killed."

"This is all I got left," the owner said. "I'm not lettin' a bunch of cycle goons take it away."

Judd watched Red get off his bike and grab Pete by the hair. He jerked it back from his face and pointed. The others laughed.

"I'm not lettin' him die out there," the owner said, heading for the door.

"Wait!" Judd shouted. "Let it play out."

Red let go and stepped back. Pete seemed animated, gesturing and talking loudly. A few bikers stared at him. Others shook their heads and laughed.

Judd froze. He knew the danger outside, but he couldn't let Pete get killed.

"I'm going out there," Judd finally said. "If we need you, I'll signal you like this." Judd scratched the back of his neck.

"Got it," the owner said. "Now be careful."

Judd opened the door slowly. Pete still talked. The bikers sat with arms folded. When Judd got close to the pumps, he heard Red say, "Since when did you become perfect? Have you forgotten what you used to do?"

"I'm not perfect," Pete said.

A woman in the group spoke up. "How 'bout you and Rosie? You two were livin' together."

"I know what Rosie and I did was wrong," Pete said. "Believe me, I'd give anything to be able to talk with her like this."

Judd couldn't figure out what Pete was doing.

Pete turned and saw Judd. He smiled and said softly, "Bet you didn't know if this Christian thing would stick with me, huh?"

"I liked the old Pete better," someone said.

"Yeah, the boozin', cussin', fightin' Pete," another said.

"Look, I don't know all the verses and everything," Pete said. "This guy does. His name's Judd. He's the one who helped me."

Red got back on his motorcycle and kicked it to a start. "Don't want your religion," he said. "And next time you get in our way, you'll pay."

The other cycles rumbled to a start and followed Red. Pete watched the trail of dust and shook his head.

"You told them about God?" Judd said.

"They need to hear it as much as I did. They don't want to hear it, though."

"You didn't want it for a lot of years," Judd said.

"Maybe someday they'll listen."

Vicki awoke to bright sunshine. A man was speaking through a bullhorn. Darrion and Shelly followed her out of the tent. Vicki felt grungy and wished she could take a shower.

"All able-bodied people should move to the media tent for a special announcement," the GC guard was saying. "Potentate Nicolae

Carpathia will make a statement via satellite shortly."

"You think he can use an earthquake for his own good?" Shelly said sarcastically.

"He'll use anything and everything," Vicki said.

The three girls reached the tent and watched a Global Community newscaster give the latest. "The number of dead and injured worldwide is staggering," the man said. "These pictures show the extent of the damage."

Video clips of major cities flashed on the screen. A shot of Paris showed the Eiffel Tower in ruins. The Leaning Tower of Pisa was no longer leaning but flat on the ground. Shots of New York, Los Angeles, and Chicago made Vicki shudder.

"Other natural phenomena occurred during the earthquake," the newscaster said. "This amateur video was shot in New Babylon during the earthquake."

Vicki gasped. The camera was shaky, but there was no mistaking the fire in the sky. The moon had turned blood red.

"No matter how much they try to explain that away," Darrion said, "we all know that the moon turning that color is not a natural phenomenon."

Nicolae Carpathia's face flashed on the

screen. He looked grim but composed. "Brothers and sisters in the Global Community, I address you from New Babylon. Like you, I lost many loved ones, dear friends, and loyal associates in the tragedy. Please accept my deepest and most sincere sympathy for your losses on behalf of the administration of the Global Community.

"No one could have predicted this random act of nature, the worst in history to strike the globe. We were in the final stages of our rebuilding effort following the war against a resistant minority. Now, as I trust you are able to witness wherever you are, rebuilding has already begun again."

Nicolae told viewers that New Babylon would become the center of the world for banking, government, and even Enigma Babylon One World Faith.

"Told you he'd use the earthquake to his own advantage," Vicki smirked.

"It will be my joy to welcome you to this beautiful place," Nicolae continued. "Give us a few months to finish, and then plan your pilgrimage. Every citizen should make it his or her life's goal to experience this new utopia and see the prototype for every city."

The screen switched from Nicolae to a virtual reality tour of the new city. It gleamed, as if already completed. The tour was dizzying and impressive. Carpathia pointed out every high-tech, state-of-the-art convenience.

"Looks pretty impressive," Shelly said.

"It's a fake," Vicki said. "The guy can only attempt to copy what God does."

The potentate continued with a stirring pep talk. "Because you are survivors, I have unwavering confidence in your drive and determination and commitment to work together, to never give up, to stand shoulder to shoulder and rebuild our world.

"I am humbled to serve you and pledge that I will give my all for as long as you allow me the privilege. Now let me just add that I am aware that, due to speculative reporting in one of our own Global Community publications, many have been confused by recent events."

"What's he talking about?" Shelly said.

"Must be Buck Williams's magazine article," Vicki said.

"While it may appear that the global earthquake coincided with the so-called wrath of the Lamb, let me clarify," Nicolae said. "Those who believe this disaster was God's doing are also those who believe that the disappearances nearly two years ago were people being swept away to heaven.

"Of course, every citizen of the Global Community is free to believe as he or she wants and to exercise that faith in any way that does not infringe upon the same freedom for others. The point of Enigma Babylon One World Faith is religious freedom and tolerance.

"For that reason, I am loath to criticize the beliefs of others. However, I plead for common sense. I do not begrudge anyone the right to believe in a personal god."

"Gee, thanks," Darrion muttered.

"However, I do not understand how a god they describe as just and loving would capriciously decide who is or is not worthy of heaven and effect that decision in what they refer to as 'the twinkling of an eye.'

"Has this same loving god come back two years later to rub it in? He expresses his anger to those unfortunates left behind by laying waste their world and killing off a huge percentage of them?"

"Look at that smile," Vicki said. "Makes me sick."

"I humbly ask devout believers in such a Supreme Being to forgive me if I have mischaracterized your god," Carpathia continued. "But any thinking citizen realizes that this picture simply does not add up.

"So, my brothers and sisters, do not blame God for what we are enduring. See it simply as one of life's crucibles, a test of our spirit and will, an opportunity to look within ourselves and draw on that deep wellspring of goodness we were born with. Let us work together to make our world a global phoenix, rising from the ashes of tragedy to become the greatest society ever known. I bid you good-bye and goodwill until next I speak with you."

People around the tent stood and clapped. Vicki shook her head and remained seated. When the others sat, Vicki recognized a familiar face.

"Isn't that the guy who was at Judd's graduation?" Shelly said.

"Leon Fortunato," Vicki said.

Fortunato seemed friendly and looked straight into the camera. "I want to tell you an incredible story," he said. "So incredible that I would not believe it if it had not happened to me.

"I was in the top floor offices of the Global Community when the earthquake hit. Unlike the potentate, I was unable to escape. But I am glad he did, because if it were not for him, I would be dead.

"The building collapsed around us," Leon continued. "I wish I could say I was brave during this time, but like the rest, I went screaming into the rubble. I fell headfirst, and when I hit the bottom, it felt and sounded like I'd cracked my skull. The weight of the whole building came down on me, breaking my bones. My lungs burst. Everything went black."

Fortunato stopped. Vicki watched the crowd in the tent. They were leaning forward, listening to every word.

"I believe I died," Fortunato said. "It was as if someone pulled the plug on my life."

Another pause. "And yet, here I am. Alive. You ask me how? I say it was my friend Nicolae. I was not conscious of anything, like the deepest sleep a person could ever have. And then I heard a voice calling my name. I thought it was a dream. I thought I was a boy again and my mother was softly calling my name, trying to wake me from sleep.

"Then I heard the loud, strong voice of your potentate. He cried out, 'Leonardo, come forth!' "

"I don't believe it," Vicki said.

"What?" Darrion said.

"Those are the same words Jesus used with Lazarus to bring him back from the dead," Vicki said.

A woman turned in front of the girls and shushed them.

Leon Fortunato wiped his brow and composed himself. "I'm sorry for being emotional," he said. "My only regret was that there were no witnesses. But I know what I experienced and believe with all my heart that this gift our Supreme Potentate possesses will be used in public in the future. A man bestowed with this power is worthy of a new title. I am suggesting that he hereafter be referred to as His Excellency Nicolae Carpathia. I have already instituted this policy within the Global Community government and urge all citizens who respect and love our leader to follow suit.

"As you may know, His Excellency would never require or even request such a title. Though reluctantly thrust into leadership, he has expressed a willingness to give his life for his fellow citizens. Though he will never insist upon appropriate deference, I urge it on your part."

"That's all I can take," Vicki said. "Come on."

Outside the tent, Shelly asked Vicki what she thought of Leon Fortunato's statement.

"Look," Vicki said, "God does miracles; there's no question. All the enemy of God can do is copy the miracles. He fakes it. With

the mind control Carpathia has, I wouldn't
be surprised if he planted those thoughts
about Fortunato being raised from the
dead."

"But you heard him yourself," Shelly said.
"He climbed out from the bottom of that
building."

"Right," Vicki said, "and he claimed to
have broken all kinds of bones and burst his
lungs. Did those just heal over?"

Darrion spoke up. "The point isn't whether
it's true or not," she said. "People are going
to believe it. They're going to think Carpathia
is some kind of Messiah himself."

Lionel and the others watched the speeches
by Carpathia and Fortunato. Several out-
bursts of clapping and cheering were stopped
by Commander Blancka. When it was
over, the group rose to its feet. Everyone but
Conrad.

"What's the matter with you?" Lionel said.

Conrad shook his head. "I'm just not in
the rah-rah mood," he said.

"Didn't you hear?" Lionel said. "Carpathia
actually raised somebody from the dead.
Don't you know what that means?"

"Yeah, a new GC health care plan. Somebody dies, and Nicolae brings them to life again."

"You don't get it," Lionel said.

"I do get it," Conrad said. "I just have a hard time believing it. Let me ask you this. There were other dead people in that building who worked with Carpathia. If he's the wonderful leader everybody thinks he is, why did he only raise one person from the dead? Why not the whole bunch?"

Lionel stammered. He hadn't thought of that angle. Finally, he said, "You have to decide whether you're in or out."

Conrad shook his head. "I'm in. But only until I can find my brother."

It was evening when Judd and Pete neared New Hope Village Church. As Pete drove his motorcycle over chunks of asphalt and concrete, Judd looked at what once was a beautiful place of worship. Now, half the building was underground. The entire sanctuary appeared to have turned and was sitting at a weird angle.

The last time Judd had been in the church was at Bruce's funeral. How his life had changed since then. Now he was on the run from the Global Community.

"This is where my new life really started," Judd said. "After the disappearances, I met Bruce here."

"It's a shame. Looks like it was quite a church."

Judd got off the cycle and looked around the parking lot. Loretta's place was not far. He wondered if she was alive. And Vicki. Where could she be?

Pete broke Judd's silence. "I'm glad you made it back, and I hope you find what you're looking for."

"You're leaving?" Judd said.

"I want to check on that old guy at the gas station. We never got to tell him what you told me."

"You need to study and get grounded," Judd said. "Stay here."

"Can't. I have a few loose ends to tie and lots of people who need to hear what I know."

Judd put out his hand. "I hope this won't be the last time we see each other."

"It won't be," Pete said. "You can count on it."

EIGHT

Reunion

AFTER an overnight stay in Indianapolis, Lionel and Conrad continued their flight to Chicago with Felicia and Melinda. Commander Blancka talked with his staff as they neared Glenview Naval Air Station.

Conrad tapped Lionel on the shoulder and motioned toward the commander. "Looks like something's up."

When they landed, the four kids hopped out, grabbed their belongings, and moved away from the chopper. A few minutes later Commander Blancka rushed up to them.

"We have a situation. I know you're prepared to work behind the scenes, but we need your help."

"What's up?" Lionel said.

"Looters. They're goin' wild. The GC

needs all the help they can get. Are you up for it?"

"You bet, sir," Lionel said.

The others agreed. Commander Blancka told them to stay in radio contact and passed them to another GC officer. The man scoffed when he saw the kids. Commander Blancka bristled, and the guard escorted the four to a helipad. The chopper flew over a crumpled tollway and a river.

Conrad pointed to their left. "O'Hare's over there," he said. "Not much of it left."

They passed a forest preserve, then landed in a crumpled parking lot. A crooked sign said Woodfield Mall. The upper level of the huge building had collapsed. Several stores on the lower levels were intact. Lionel and the others walked over broken glass to get inside. Empty shelves and overturned tables littered store floors. The looters had done a job.

The guard stepped through water from a broken fountain and met another GC patrol. "I didn't know we were getting a bunch of kids," he muttered.

"You heard the commander," Lionel said. "We know what we're doing."

"If you four can contain this area," the patrol said, "it'll give the rest of us a chance to work some other problem spots."

"What happens if we see somebody stealing something?" Melinda said.

The guard rolled his eyes. "You could try to talk them out of it," the guard said, "but our orders are to shoot. I suggest you do the same."

Judd slept near New Hope Village Church. He awoke stiff and cold. The nearest house was Loretta's. He could tell someone had dug through the roof to get inside. A few garden tools lay at the back of the house. He shouted but no one answered.

He was amazed to find an empty crater where his own house had been. A meteor had struck it, and nothing was left but debris and the huge hole. In an open field he found the swing set he and his father had put together for his little brother and sister. Concrete was still attached to the foot of each post.

Judd bent to inspect the swings and found what he was looking for. He had written his initials in the concrete. On another leg of the swings he saw his little brother's handprint. Over it he had written "Marc." He saw the same on the next leg where Marcie had written her name and pushed her hand deep into the cement.

Judd knelt and inspected the last post. It was chipped, but he could still make out the letters "Da—." Judd put his hand in the imprint of his father's hand and closed his eyes. Judd's hand almost fit perfectly.

"I wish you were here now, Dad," Judd said. He thought of his father, brother, and sister. It seemed so long ago, like another world. It *was* another world.

Judd thought of his other family. Lionel, Ryan, Vicki, and Bruce. Judd guessed Ryan and Lionel would have stayed at his house. That would explain why Ryan was listed as dead. But how would Lionel have gotten away? Judd still held out hope for Ryan as he traced his way back to the church. After several wrong turns, he found the rubble of Vicki's place.

"Halt!" someone behind him shouted.

Judd turned to see a Global Community squad in a covered vehicle. "What are you doing?"

Judd knew the GC would shoot if he ran. He played it cool. "Looking for some friends of mine," Judd shouted.

"This area's been evacuated," a man said. "Check the shelters."

Judd gave a sigh of relief when the GC squad drove past him.

After the men flew away in the chopper, Lionel and the others paced in front of the darkened windows. One jewelry shop was completely gutted. Another that sold fine luggage had nothing left but some boxes high on the wall. Escalators tilted, and the silence was eerie.

"I hear they wasted Chicago at the start of the war," Conrad said. "Now this."

"What war?" Lionel said.

Conrad told Lionel the details of the war between the Global Community and the militia. "My brother said the GC was just waiting for a militia uprising. They wanted to blow them away and make it look like the Global Community was just defending themselves."

"Who's your brother?" Felicia said.

"His name is Taylor Graham," Conrad said. "Works for Maxwell Stahley in GC security."

"Stahley's dead," Felicia said. "You haven't heard?"

Conrad looked upset. "He was alive when they took me down South," Conrad said. "Was it a plane crash?"

"They found him in a building in some suburb," Felicia said.

Lionel held up a hand. The four stood in front of an upscale dress shop. "Somebody's in there," Lionel said.

"I see some things I wouldn't mind wearing," Melinda said. "But I don't see any looters."

Lionel climbed through the broken window. Glass crunched under his feet. He heard shuffling inside.

"Come on!" Lionel shouted to his friends. Lionel cupped his hands and yelled, "Halt! In the name of the Global Community, or we'll shoot."

"I'll cut through the next store and meet you in the back," Conrad whispered.

Melinda and Felicia were right behind Lionel, hurtling past the racks of expensive clothes. Lionel hit the ground and saw two people running for the rear exit.

"Stop right there or we'll shoot!" Lionel repeated.

The two kept running. Lionel pointed the gun to the ceiling and shot. Melinda screamed and lost her balance, sending Lionel headlong into a display.

"Are you OK?" Felicia said, helping Lionel up.

"Yeah," Lionel said, but he wasn't. He had a welt under his ear, and something was going on in his head. Things were coming

back. About Chicago. About his life before
the Global Community.

Vicki, Shelly, and Darrion were busy at the
shelter. Vicki could tell the nurses appreci-
ated the help. Hundreds of people poured in
each day. Some were looking for a meal.
Others were injured and needed medical
help.

Vicki didn't want to think about the future.
Each question made her stomach tie in
knots. Where would they live? What would
they do for money? She tried to concentrate
and push the questions out of her mind, but
they kept coming back.

Vicki heard Shelly shout first. Then
Darrion called her name. Vicki asked the
woman she was helping to stay where she
was. She stepped out of the medical tent and
spotted Darrion and Shelly. Both were smiling. Behind them was a man in dirty jeans
with a few days' growth of beard.

"Vick," the man said.

"Judd?"

Judd ran to her. Vicki hugged him tightly.

"I've been looking all over," Judd said.
"I'm so glad I found you."

"The GC wouldn't tell us anything. How'd you get away?"

"Long story," Judd said. "Is there someplace we can talk?"

Shelly winked at Vicki and said she would take over in the medical tent. Vicki and Judd walked toward the church.

Lionel ran out the back door, his head pounding. Felicia and Melinda were behind him. Lionel went from the darkened back room to bright sunlight. When his eyes adjusted, he saw two men struggling with Conrad. Lionel pointed the gun but couldn't get a clear shot. Before he could reach his friend, one of the men had wrestled the gun from Conrad.

"Stay right there if you want to live," the man said.

"Put the gun down," Lionel said.

"Yeah, right," the man said. "Who do you kids think you are anyway, the cops?"

"We're with the Global Community," Lionel said, keying the microphone on his shoulder. He gave their position and requested help.

"That was a mistake," the man with the gun said. He leveled the gun at Lionel.

Lionel fired at the knee of the gunman. The man stared at him, then shook his head. To Lionel's surprise, the man dropped the gun and walked toward the parking lot. Lionel knew he couldn't have missed, but the man kept walking.

Conrad scampered to retrieve the gun.

"Stay where you are!" Lionel yelled.

The men kept walking. Lionel heard a chopper. Above the building he saw Commander Blancka give him a thumbs-up. Lionel motioned toward the men, but the commander ignored him. The chopper landed nearby, and the commander jumped out.

"They're getting away, sir," Lionel said.

"No, they're not," Commander Blancka said. "They're being debriefed."

"What's going on?" Conrad said.

"It's one thing to know how to fire a gun and hit a target," the commander said. "It's another to use it against a person."

"You mean that whole thing was staged?" Melinda said.

"Our guns were loaded with blanks," Lionel said.

"It was your last test, and you passed," the commander said.

Conrad looked depressed. "I don't think I did very well."

"We put you in a situation you weren't prepared for," Commander Blancka said. "Hopefully you learned something."

The commander ushered them to the chopper. "Here's where we have you set up," he said, pointing to a map. "Mount Prospect is just east of us. We're putting all four of you there. We've heard reports of some resistance in the high school.

"As I told you, school as you've known it won't exist in the coming months. What we hope you'll do is get situated and blend in with the community."

"Where will we stay?" Lionel said.

"Just like everybody else who lives there," the commander said. "You'll stay in a shelter until homes and apartments can be rebuilt."

Judd told Vicki about the earthquake and watching Taylor Graham fall to his death. It felt like Judd could tell her anything. He explained about the mark of true believers, and Vicki gasped when she saw the mark on Judd's forehead.

"You're right," Vicki said. "We all have the mark."

Vicki listened and asked questions about

Pete and how Judd made it home. "You're lucky to be alive," she said.

"I feel like God's been watching out for me the whole time. What happened with you?"

Vicki explained about the *Underground* and how Mrs. Jenness had caught her. Judd couldn't believe Vicki's ordeal on the bridge.

"And I thought I had it tough," Judd said. "What about Lionel and Ryan?"

Vicki looked away.

Judd took her by the shoulders and looked into her eyes. "I read something on a Web site, but I want to hear it from you. Is Ryan dead?"

Vicki pursed her lips. "I feel like it's my fault. I told him to stay in the house. If he'd have been outside maybe he'd still be alive."

"Then he is dead?"

"They found him in the basement of my house. His back was hurt, and he had some kind of infection."

Vicki's voice broke. She put her head on Judd's shoulder. "I found him at a makeshift hospital. He'd written me a note the night before."

"Do you still have it?" Judd said.

Vicki pulled the crumpled piece of paper

from her back pocket. "I got to talk with him before he died."

Judd opened the paper. He wiped away a tear as he read it, then sat on a fallen tree. "It doesn't seem real," he said.

"I had to get help bringing his body here." She pointed to the church. Judd saw a fresh mound of earth. Phoenix was perched on top.

Judd walked slowly toward the grave, then knelt beside it and stroked the dog's back. Phoenix whimpered and put his head on Judd's knee.

"It's not your fault," Judd said to Vicki. "You were just trying to protect him from the GC."

"But he died! And he's never coming back!"

Judd sat with the feeling. First his family. Then Bruce. Now it was Ryan. Judd kept seeing Ryan's face. He had called him a little guy for so long. He thought of Ryan's fights with Lionel, his love for Phoenix, and their trip to Israel together. That trip had shown Judd what Ryan was made of.

"You haven't told me about Lionel."

"Somebody from his family came and took him down South," Vicki said.

"I thought his family was gone," Judd said.

"Apparently a few of them were living and

wanted him home. We haven't heard
anything since he left."

"Weird," Judd said.

"At least you're back," Vicki said.

"But I don't know how long I can stay,"
Judd said. "The GC network will be up and
running soon. The first place they'll look will
be here. I think we need a permanent place
to hide."

"You must be starving," Vicki said. "Let's
go back to the shelter."

"Gimme a minute with him, OK?" Judd
said.

Vicki walked to the edge of the parking lot
while Judd put a hand on Ryan's grave.

"I feel real stupid," Judd said. "I mean, I
know you can't hear me. So this is probably
more for me than it is you.

"I'm sorry. Sorry I treated you like a kid.
You were the best of us. You loved God with
everything you had. You went out and found
those Bibles. You saved me and Vicki that
time under the L tracks.

"I'm gonna miss you. And it hurts like
everything to let you go. But I know I have to
say good-bye. I just wish I could see you one
more time and tell you. . . .

"You were like . . . no, you *were* my

brother. You are my brother. And I'm gonna see you again."

Vicki patted Judd on the back when he walked back to her. "I've done that a couple of times myself."

They moved toward the shelter. Judd said he would sleep outside near a fire. When they reached camp, Vicki relieved Shelly in the medical tent. As Vicki helped an elderly patient roll over, someone in the corner shouted, "That's her!"

Vicki finished with the patient and hurried to see what the problem was. Vicki finally realized the girl was talking about her.

"Nurse, get a guard," the girl said. "She's the one. That's the girl who killed Mrs. Jenness!"

NINE

Accused

VICKI was stunned. It wasn't true, but there was no way to prove her innocence. Anyone who might have seen her trying to rescue Mrs. Jenness could easily have thought she was trying to get rid of the woman.

A nurse came and quieted the shouting girl.

"I'm telling you, she's the one who offed Mrs. Jenness."

The nurse looked at Vicki. "Do you mind telling me what this is about?"

Shelly whispered to Vicki, "That's Joyce from Nicolae High. Let me see what I can do."

Vicki finally recognized her. Shelly tried to calm her, but Joyce kept shouting and calling Vicki a murderer.

"Were you in a car with Mrs. Jenness?" the nurse said.

"Yes. The earthquake hit as we were crossing a bridge. But I tried to save her, not kill her."

Joyce spoke up. "I was there when Mrs. Jenness drove away with you. I know you were in that car. This morning I met a lady who was near the bridge when it collapsed. She described Mrs. Jenness's car perfectly and said when it went in the water there was a girl on top trying to push Mrs. Jenness back inside."

"That's not true!" Vicki said.

"She killed her!"

"I was trying to save her life."

"Calm down," the nurse said.

"I want a GC guard notified right now," Joyce said. "She's a murderer!"

Vicki saw Judd talking to a woman in the corner. A moment later the woman walked up and demanded silence. Vicki saw a smudge on her forehead. "There will be no more fighting about this." The woman looked at Vicki. "You go back to your tent."

"If you won't do anything about it," Joyce shouted, "I'm going to the authorities!"

"Give her something to calm her," the woman said.

"No!" Joyce shouted as the nurse grabbed a needle. "I'll get you for this, Byrne!"

Lionel and the others were flown to Mount Prospect by helicopter. They checked in at a shelter but were turned away.

"Head over to Nicolae High," a worker said. "They have more room there."

"That's where we're supposed to wind up anyway," Conrad said.

While walking, Lionel looked for anything familiar. The streets and buildings were a mess. But the incident at the mall had stirred him. He now recalled the GC attack on Chicago. He remembered the day it happened and the sound of the bombers overhead. The explosions. The fear he had as he listened. But he couldn't remember the people, and he knew the people were the most important part of the puzzle.

"Do you still have those diaries?" Lionel asked Conrad.

"Didn't have room to pack them," Conrad said. "I brought your Bible, though. Been reading it."

Lionel looked at the inscription in the Bible as he walked. *Who is Ryan?* Lionel thought. *And what does he have to do with all this?*

"You think you're gonna find your friends?" Conrad said.

"The thought's crossed my mind," Lionel said.

When they neared Nicolae High, Lionel stopped the others. "We have to be careful not to come on too strong. We don't want to try and impress people with how important we are."

"Is that what you think we want to do?" Felicia said.

"I'm not saying—"

"You're not the boss of everybody," Melinda interrupted. She rolled her eyes.

"Like it or not, the commander put me in charge," Lionel said. "And I want it understood. We might not have anything to report for months. It's like going undercover."

"Give us some credit," Felicia said. "We went through the training too."

They walked in silence to Nicolae High. Lionel talked with a staff worker. "This place has been turned into a morgue," the man said. "We've had a hard time keeping track of all the bodies."

"Where are people staying?" Conrad said.

"We have four shelters in the area," the man said, pointing them out on a crudely drawn map. "Get to any of these and you'll find food and a place to stay warm."

"Are any teachers or administrators of the school still around?" Lionel asked.

"Plenty of them. They're under all those sheets."

Judd called a meeting of the Young Trib Force that evening. He commended Vicki, Shelly, and Darrion for the way they had handled themselves during the past few days.

"It's clear we need a place to hide," Judd said. "The GC will be looking for me, and this thing with Joyce could blow up in Vicki's face."

"What's the deal with her anyway?" Darrion said.

"I knew her from school," Shelly said. "After the disappearances, we hung out together. When I became a Christian, she turned on me."

"I remember talking with her," Vicki said. "Joyce said she believed Jesus came back. She thought it was the only explanation."

"So she's a believer?" Darrion said.

"No," Vicki said. "She said if the disappearances were God's idea of how to do things, she wanted no part of it. Then she told me not to waste my breath trying to convince her."

"So she's chosen not to believe," Darrion said.

"Exactly," Vicki said.

"That may be why she's trying to pin murder on you," Judd said. "She must hate anything that reminds her of the truth."

Judd put together a list of people they knew who were missing or dead. They were all concerned about John and Mark. Vicki asked Judd to explain what he knew about the mark on their foreheads.

Judd noticed a strange young man walking toward them.

"Vicki!" Charlie shouted. "They kicked me out. Boom, just like that, out the door, on the street, no more Charlie in the store, or hospital, or whatever it is. Said I had to find my own place to stay."

"What about the nurse?" Vicki said.

"She got in trouble," Charlie said. "Lost a patient. I think it was that kid I carried for you."

"Oh, no," Vicki said.

"Oh yeah," Charlie said. "They kicked me out and told me not to come back."

Vicki introduced Charlie to the rest of the group. Charlie shook hands with Judd, but his hand was limp.

"What're you guys looking at each other's heads for?" Charlie said.

Judd looked at Vicki. Vicki shrugged.

"We're talking about . . . something that we all have in common," Judd said.

"You're in a club?" Charlie said. "Can I be in too?"

"Well," Judd said, "it's not really a club. It's more like—"

"You guys look like friends," Charlie said. "Happy. I want to join. Now what's with your head?"

"We all have a mark," Vicki said. "It means we're for real."

Charlie squinted at Vicki and looked her over. "You guys are crazy. There's nothin' on your head."

"You can't see it," Vicki said. "Only those who believe can see it."

"This is really weird," Charlie said.

Judd wondered if they were telling Charlie too much. He took Vicki aside.

"He's the one who helped me carry Ryan," Vicki said.

"I just don't want to take a chance and tell him stuff that might get us in trouble."

"How can we keep it from him? Isn't that why we're here?"

"Of course it is, but we have to make sure we can trust the people we tell."

"Oh yeah," Vicki said, "I haven't seen that in the Bible lately. Besides, you were talking about this stuff to a woman who's with Enigma Babylon One World Faith."

"She was asking questions," Judd said. "I had no choice."

"Charlie's asking questions too."

Charlie interrupted and pointed to Shelly. "That girl says if I believe like you guys, I get something on my head too. Can I get it now, or do I have to pay something?"

Lionel and Conrad unpacked two tents the Global Community had given them while Melinda and Felicia checked out the shelter for food.

"Recognize anything around here?" Conrad said.

Lionel was cautious. "Some stuff came back about the war when we were at the mall, but none of this looks familiar."

"How about the high school?" Conrad said.

Lionel shook his head.

"It was pretty messed up. Maybe we'll find somebody who knew you."

Felicia and Melinda were out of breath when they returned.

"Where's the food?" Lionel said.

"Just got a lead on something," Felicia said. "I met a girl in the medical tent who says somebody committed a murder during the earthquake."

"That's out of our league," Conrad said.

"The girl says the person who killed this lady is one of those religious nuts we're supposed to be looking for," Felicia said. "And get this. The girl was accused of trying to push her beliefs on people at Nicolae High."

"Sounds like it'd be worth checking out," Conrad said.

"How'd you find this girl?" Lionel said. "She just walked up to you and spilled her guts?"

"She said nobody's listening to her," Melinda said. "I told her we were with the Global Community."

"You what?!" Lionel said.

"I didn't say we were officially with them or anything," Melinda said. "I just said we could look into it if she wanted."

Lionel shook his head. "Let's go back over there and get the story."

Judd thought Charlie seemed a little odd. Slow. He looked away when he talked to Judd, and he had a funny walk. But Vicki was right. Those things didn't disqualify him from knowing about God.

"First thing I need you to know," Judd said, "is that this isn't a club you join. Do you get that?"

"Not a club, got it. What do I have to do to get one of those things on my head?"

Judd rubbed his neck. "You can't do this just because you want a thing on your head, Charlie."

"Come on, tell me. I want to see everybody else's."

"Then we have to talk seriously about what we believe."

"Believe about what?"

"About God. About what happened to the people who disappeared."

"My sister got killed in the big shake," Charlie said.

"That's what Vicki said. I'm sorry."

"They kicked me out of the store where she worked. Told me not to come back."

"You can stay with us for a while."

"Right. So what am I supposed to believe?"

Judd sighed. "Did your sister ever take you to church?"

Lionel told the others to wait outside while he talked with Joyce. "I don't want it looking like we're here on some kind of official business."

Joyce was still groggy from the medication, but she was able to talk. She repeated her story, then added, "The girl's name is Vicki Byrne."

Lionel thought about the name. It sounded familiar.

"I was near the office when Mrs. Jenness took Vicki out to the car," Joyce said. "I know she killed her. She's probably bolted by now."

"Why would she kill your principal?" Lionel said. He wrote the name *Mrs. Jenness* on a piece of paper.

Joyce cocked her head. "Do I know you? You don't go to Nicolae High, do you?"

"Not anymore," Lionel said. "Finish your story."

"Mrs. Jenness had the goods on her. She found something and was taking Vicki away."

Lionel noticed someone on the other side of the tent. A girl with red hair was looking at him. She smiled when Lionel spotted her and waved. Then she rushed toward him.

Joyce sat up in bed and screamed, "That's her!"

The girl with red hair stopped, then turned and ran out of the tent.

Vicki was out of breath when she found
Judd. She interrupted his conversation with
Charlie. "I saw him. He's here!"

"Who?" Judd said.

"Lionel! He was in the tent talking with
Joyce."

Judd stood. "I'll be back," he said to
Charlie.

"That's good," Charlie said. "I can wait. Go
find your friend. I'm cool with that."

Judd wondered if it really was Lionel.
His heart raced as he neared the medical
tent.

"Go get her!" Joyce shouted.

"She won't get far," Lionel said.

"Your friend said you're with the Global
Community. You can do something about
her, can't you?"

Lionel frowned. "Sometimes my friends
get carried away."

"But she told me if this really was a murder,
the GC would look into it. She promised."

Lionel studied Joyce. It was possible they
had been in the same hallway together
only a few weeks ago at Nicolae High. Her

locker could have been a few feet from his own.

"Don't you believe me?" Joyce said. "She's a murderer!"

TEN

The Showdown

JUDD recognized Lionel right away. Lionel wore different clothes and seemed surprised when Judd approached.

"Good to see you again," Judd said, smiling.

Lionel backed away. "Do I know you?"

"Of course you do."

Lionel paused. "Are you Ryan?"

Judd laughed. "This is a joke, right? It's Judd, remember?"

"That guy was in on it too," Joyce said. "Judd Thompson. Last year at graduation he gave this speech, and the GC—"

"I'll handle this," Lionel said. He turned to Judd. "How do I know you?"

Judd shook his head. "You stayed in my house. I drove you to school. We ate meals together. Went to church. Don't you remember any of that?"

Lionel looked down. "I remember reading something about you in my diary."

Vicki couldn't stand it any longer. She didn't care about Joyce, she was going to see her friend. She rushed up and gave Lionel a hug.

"That's her," Joyce shouted. "Somebody arrest her!"

"Enough," Lionel said.

Lionel bristled and Vicki pulled away.

"What's wrong?" Vicki said.

"He doesn't remember us," Judd said.

"That's crazy," Vicki said.

"I had an accident during the earthquake. I could remember stuff about the camp, but not anything before that."

"What camp?" Vicki said. "You went down South to be with your family, didn't you?"

Lionel frowned.

"A man from your family came to our school," Vicki said. "You had a hard time deciding, but you finally went. We didn't hear any more from you."

"I demand you do something," Joyce said.

Lionel held up a hand. "Give me a minute to think, OK?"

Lionel walked away. Images and thoughts swirled in his head. The school. A man taking him to a seedy hotel in Chicago. A van ride. Getting chased through a swamp. It was all coming back slowly and in pieces.

But Lionel also saw Commander Blancka's stern face. Lionel had pledged to serve the Global Community. If Joyce was telling the truth, he should report Judd and Vicki. If they were really his friends, he should help them. He felt trapped.

Judd and Vicki moved away from Joyce.

"What's going on with Lionel?" Vicki said.

"We can't worry about him. We have to figure out what's best for us. Maybe we should get out of here before something bad happens."

"And leave Lionel?" Vicki said. "No way."

Another boy joined Lionel, and the two returned. "This is Conrad," Lionel said.

Judd stared at the boy. He recalled Taylor Graham talking about a brother named Conrad.

"What's your last name?" Judd said.

"Why do you want to know?"

"Is it Graham?"

Conrad looked startled, then composed himself. "How'd you know that?"

"I knew your brother," Judd said.

Conrad's eyes widened. "You knew Taylor? How is he?"

Lionel held up a hand. "You can talk later. Right now I want to get to the bottom of the murder question."

"You don't actually believe her, do you?" Vicki said.

"I don't know what to believe," Lionel said. "Step outside the tent. I want to get more information."

Vicki walked away with Lionel. Joyce shouted behind them. "Why are you taking information? Are you some kind of police officer?"

"I'm a citizen of the Global Community like you," Lionel said.

Vicki took Lionel by the shoulders. "Look at me. You're talking crazy. Don't you remember? Your mother worked for *Global Weekly*. Then your whole family disappeared. I knew your sister, Clarice. We rode the bus together."

Lionel put away his notebook and pen.

"You and I met Bruce on the same day," Vicki said.

"Go back," Lionel said. "Tell me more about my family."

Judd walked outside with Conrad.

"You really knew my brother?" Conrad said.

"I'll tell you about your brother if you'll tell me about Lionel," Judd said.

Conrad nodded. "We've spent the last few weeks in a Global Community camp down South. They trained us to become GC Morale Monitors."

"Morale Monitors?" Judd said.

"We're supposed to blend in and report anyone suspicious to the GC command."

"Suspicious?"

"Yeah, like religious fanatics who talk about Jesus coming back," Conrad said.

Judd scowled. "Why doesn't he remember us?"

"Probably a combination of the mind control the GC used and the fact that he got conked on the head. Pretty much wiped out his hard drive, if you know what I mean. Before the accident, he was talking about going along with the GC program until he could get back up here to his friends. Now he's pretty much following them lockstep."

"Why are you telling me this? You're one of them, right?"

Conrad glanced about. "I've been reading Lionel's Bible and some of the materials he brought with him. I even got on the Internet and found that rabbi's Web site. I want to know more."

The more Lionel listened, the more sense Vicki made. His family had disappeared and left him behind.

"Didn't I have a relative?" Lionel said. "A guy?"

"Uncle André."

"Yeah," Lionel said. He closed his eyes as Vicki continued.

"He's dead. He had a run-in with some bad guys. That's when Judd took us all into his house. We had meetings just about every day with our pastor, Bruce Barnes."

Lionel shook his head, his eyes still shut. "I'm not remembering any of that."

"You and Ryan used to fight like cats and do—"

"Who did you say?"

"Ryan. You and Ryan used to fight over the stupidest things."

"Where is he?" Lionel said.

"Come with me," Vicki said.

Judd told Conrad the story of meeting Taylor Graham and flying to Israel. "We didn't know it at the time, but your brother was trying to protect you."

"He knew I was being held."

"Yes, but he protected us too. He was a good man."

"Was?"

"I can't be sure, but I think your brother didn't make it through the earthquake."

Conrad frowned. Judd described Taylor's fall into the gorge. It was the last Judd saw of him.

"If anybody could survive that, it's my brother," Conrad said. "Where'd Lionel and the girl go?"

Lionel sensed Vicki and Judd were telling the truth. In the back of his mind he saw Commander Blancka. The man would want to know everything. If Lionel contacted them, it would only be minutes before the GC converged on them.

"Do you know those two following us?" Vicki said.

Lionel turned and saw Melinda and Felicia. "They're in our group."

When they reached the church, Vicki led Lionel to Ryan's grave. Phoenix still stood watch, jumping up and growling when the group drew closer.

"Ryan's name was in my Bible," Lionel said.

"He found a bunch of them and gave you one. This is his dog, Phoenix. He named him that because—"

"—because he found him in the ashes," Lionel said.

"You remember?"

"No, just the story about the bird rising." Lionel kicked at the dirt around the grave. "Maybe if I saw his face. Do you have a picture?"

Vicki took Lionel by the shoulders again. "Look at my forehead. Do you see that mark?"

Lionel shook his head. "I've already looked. I don't have that on my head."

"You do," Vicki said. "I can see it. Look at my forehead."

Lionel squinted, leaned closer, and said, "Yeah, it looks like a bruise or a smudge."

"When you asked God to come into your

life, he sealed you. This is the sign of that seal. He's not gonna let you go because you bumped your head."

Lionel put his head in his hands and sat on the grave. "This is too much."

"Do you believe me?" Vicki said.

"It doesn't matter whether I do or don't. I have to file a report."

"You don't have to. Think about it. If we're really enemies of the GC and you're our friend, you're an enemy of the GC."

"What if you're lying?"

"Why would I?"

"To get out of the murder rap."

"It's Joyce's word against mine," Vicki said. "You can't believe her."

"Not true," Felicia said, coming up behind them. "We found the other witness."

"Where?" Lionel said.

"At the next shelter," Felicia said. "She told us she saw Vicki on top of Mrs. Jenness's car, trying to push her under the water. And it worked. The woman's dead. They just found her car this morning. Her body's still in it."

"What are you going to do, Lionel?" Melinda said.

"Just leave us alone a minute, OK?"

Melinda and Felicia walked away. Lionel rammed his fist into the grave. Phoenix barked and jumped up. His ears stood straight.

Lionel pulled Vicki close. "If I turn you in and you really are my friends, I'll have betrayed you. And I'll have betrayed the memory of my friend."

Lionel grabbed a fistful of dirt and held it in his hand. Judd and Conrad came close.

"You have to believe them," Conrad whispered to Lionel.

Lionel rubbed his eyes. Images flashed through his brain. A boy on a bike riding next to him. Running through a school hallway at night.

Lionel looked up. "We fought about something, didn't we?"

"You and Ryan fought about everything," Judd said.

"We were putting something in the back of a car," Lionel said, his eyes darting back and forth. "The other kid grabbed me around the neck and wrestled me to the ground."

"You were loading Bibles," Judd said. "I had to separate you."

"He had a stash somewhere. . . ." Lionel said, his voice quickening. "He'd go off and wouldn't come back for hours."

"We found it in the church," Vicki said. "Hundreds of them were stacked up in there."

". . . and the man showed us a tape . . . Bruce . . . it was right in there that I finally understood about God. . . ."

Lionel felt the emotion rising. Things were getting clearer, like a blindfold suddenly lifting. The closeness of his friends had brought everything back.

Lionel looked at Judd. "The rabbi?"

"We don't know where he is," Judd said, "but we assume he survived the quake."

Vicki handed Lionel the note Ryan had written. Lionel scanned it, then fell beside the grave of his friend. "I wasn't here for him."

Melinda and Felicia returned. "Excuse us, but we've got a situation here," Melinda said, pointing to Vicki and Judd. "She's accused of murder, and there's evidence he's against the Global Community."

"There's no way Vicki would have killed Mrs. Jenness," Lionel said.

"Are you taking their side?" Felicia said.

"I just want to sort this thing out," Lionel said.

"Let them explain their case to Commander Blancka," Melinda said.

"I'm not reporting anything until—"

Lionel was interrupted by the *thwock-*

thwock-thwock of rotor blades. He could hear the chopper but couldn't see it yet.

"We filed a report a few minutes ago," Melinda said.

Lionel looked at Vicki and Judd. The memories were flooding back now. He was finally home, finally back with the people he loved. And they were in more danger than they had ever been in before.

ABOUT THE AUTHORS

Jerry B. Jenkins (www.jerryjenkins.com) is the writer of the Left Behind series. He is author of more than one hundred books, of which eleven have reached the *New York Times* best-seller list. Former vice president for publishing for the Moody Bible Institute of Chicago, he also served many years as editor of *Moody* magazine and is now Moody's writer-at-large.

His writing has appeared in publications as varied as *Reader's Digest, Parade,* in-flight magazines, and many Christian periodicals. He has written books in four genres: biography, marriage and family, fiction for children, and fiction for adults.

Jenkins's biographies include books with Hank Aaron, Bill Gaither, Luis Palau, Walter Payton, Orel Hershiser, Nolan Ryan, Brett Butler, and Billy Graham, among many others.

Eight of his apocalyptic novels—*Left Behind, Tribulation Force, Nicolae, Soul Harvest, Apollyon, Assassins, The Indwelling,* and *The Mark*—have appeared on the Christian Booksellers Association's best-selling fiction list and the *Publishers Weekly* religion best-seller list. *Left Behind* was nominated for Book of the Year by the Evangelical Christian Publishers Association in 1997, 1998, 1999, and 2000. *The Indwelling* was number one on the *New York Times* best-seller list for four consecutive weeks.

As a marriage and family author and speaker, Jenkins has been a frequent guest on Dr. James Dobson's *Focus on the Family* radio program.

Jerry is also the writer of the nationally syndicated sports story comic strip *Gil Thorp,* distributed to newspapers across the United States by Tribune Media Services.

Jerry and his wife, Dianna, live in Colorado.

Dr. Tim LaHaye (www.timlahaye.com), who conceived the idea of fictionalizing an account of the Rapture and the Tribulation, is a noted author, minister, and nationally recognized speaker on Bible prophecy. He is the founder of both Tim LaHaye Ministries and The Pre-Trib Research Center. Presently Dr. LaHaye speaks at many of the major Bible prophecy conferences in the U.S. and Canada, where his nine current prophecy books are very popular.

Dr. LaHaye holds a doctor of ministry degree from Western Theological Seminary and the doctor of literature degree from Liberty University. For twenty-five years he pastored one of the nation's outstanding churches in San Diego, which grew to three locations. It was during that time that he founded two accredited Christian high schools, a Christian school system of ten schools, and Christian Heritage College.

Dr. LaHaye has written over forty books, with over 30 million copies in print in thirty-three languages. He has written books on a wide variety of subjects, such as family life, temperaments, and Bible prophecy. His current fiction works, written with Jerry Jenkins—*Left Behind, Tribulation Force, Nicolae, Soul Harvest, Apollyon, Assassins, The Indwelling,* and *The Mark*—have all reached number one on the Christian best-seller charts. Other works by Dr. LaHaye are *Spirit-Controlled Temperament; How to Be Happy Though Married; Revelation Unveiled; Understanding the Last Days; Rapture under Attack; Are We Living in the End Times?;* and the youth fiction series Left Behind: The Kids.

He is the father of four grown children and grandfather of nine. Snow skiing, waterskiing, motorcycling, golfing, vacationing with family, and jogging are among his leisure activities.

The Future Is Clear

Check out the exciting Left Behind: The Kids series

BOOKS #19 AND #20 COMING SOON!